I0593880

SAVAGE ANESTHESIA

LELAND PITTS-GONZALEZ

PRAISE FOR
SAVAGE ANESTHESIA

"You know that homeless guy on the bus who sidles up to you and begins to mumble about aliens? Savage Anesthesia is what you might get if he tied you up and made you listen to him long enough that he began to make sense. Obscene and surreal, these are mindscapes to get lost in."
—Brian Evenson, author of *A Collapse of Horses*

"A work of stark and strange realism about a wholle unreal place: our very own world, which has rarely been reported on with such piercing focus. An original, paranoid, intense book of stories."
—Ben Marcus, author of *Leaving the Sea*

"Leland Pitts-Gonzalez does not transport the reader to another headspace so much as he transforms the reader. After coming out of Savage Anesthesia, looking at words, thoughts, or people in the same light is an impossibility. To say that this is addictively irreverent is an understatement."
—John Edward Lawson, author of *Bibliophile*

CB555-09: Savage Anesthesia
ISBN: 978-0-9962768-4-9

Carrion Blue 555
Chicopee MA / Lambertville NJ
carrionblue555@gmail.com

Cover art by Jim DuBois.
jimduboisart.blogspot.com
Cover design copyright ©2017 by Matthew Revert.
www.matthewrevert.com
Carrion Blue 555 logo designed by Brent Carpentier.

Savage Anesthesia copyright ©2017 by Leland Pitts-Gonzalez.

All rights reserved. No part of this book may be reproduced or transmitted in any form or by any means, electronic or mechanical, including photocopying, recording, or by any information storage and retrieval system, without the written consent of the publisher, except where permitted by law.

All persons in this book are fictitious, and any resemblance that may seem to exist to actual persons living or dead is purely coincidental or for purposes of satire or parody. All content is original to the author or included under fair use. All copyrights and trademarks are reserved by their respectful owners. This is a work of fiction.

"This is Heaven alright, but there's a man outside with a gun."
—Cardiacs, "What Paradise is Like"

TABLE OF CONTENTS

HISTORY OF THE APPARATUS

What we call the eye was once a fish. Pupils extracted oxygen from fresh water. Eyes swam in schools of a thousand or more. The optical nerve served as a tail that made a whooshing sound. They abandoned pools for banks. Off the coast of the same ecosystem, a species of kelp was the prototype for the nervous system. The spine-like kelp swayed in the current and the seminal brain was a holdfast at the brackish bottom-ledge near billions of dead cells. The gluey waste of bacterium evolved into a primitive heart. In tropical storms of that epoch, the primary skin flew through the air like a nearly infinite-spanned pollen. Over time, the epidermis wrapped around these disparate animals. It formed one organ around several lives. This primitive vertebrate burrowed in the mud and contracted a funnel-shaped virus. Without anti-bodies, the vertebrate developed hallucinations. The voices reverberated in its head. It lay with an alarming recognition of something like, "I am my own self." This is the theory that sentience was the manifestation of an infection...

There was a man and a woman. There was a vat inside the woman that repeated evolution. She had her legs up so the man could deliver the smaller one. He cupped his hands to catch it. She had many tired and stringy hairs. The smaller one came out like a fist. It yelled at the light. She gasped, "Boy or girl?" The man thought of a woman who, after having been baptized, backed into a candle. Her back lit on fire. Instead of extinguishing it, the woman jumped forward trying to leap out of herself. The man with the smaller one in his hands stared into the white, sterile wall. "It's simply material," he said to the woman.

NO MORE MAPS

I almost had trouble finding him. I went to visit my client fitted in soiled overalls and boots, thinking this might be more comforting to him. I admired the weeds tall as flagpoles around his lot (how they cloaked the street signs already with old rags). The house was cranked up on makeshift stilts, and I bent over and looked through the pallets to the back of the house where there simply were more weeds. I knocked, but there wasn't an answer, so I went past that doorframe, the sparse sunlight at his back, and saw his smelted image as he whittled branches.

I closed the distance and reached out to touch him. In his initial message, he had claimed his eyes were terminally open and that he had been born without eyelids. My palm clamped down on his shoulder and I could feel his muscles twitch, but he kept swiping away at the sticks. He looked nothing like the man who once was Supervisor and presided over the town's cartographers. He was scrawny and opened his maw with a foul odor, and his feet looked more like bony claws.

"To poke my eyes out," he said, holding one of the sharpened branches. He lifted his head and turned around to drying ferns that hung from wire by the one window, their spindly legs dangling coy and fussing up the lacy shadows.

"Always the martyr," I said. On the opposite wall was a brittle map of the town that he had revised no less than four times since that incipient sketch.

"Have you quit smoking?" he asked.

I opened my cigarette case and handed him one. He tapped the cigarette on his palm and stuck it in his mouth. I lit it for him and we sat there for a minute.

The pipes in the place croaked. He wore this T-shirt that he must've been wearing for a lifetime. It was thin and the material was already poor so that I could see through it to his nipples.

"So, I do have a chance in court?" he asked. I sat down behind him in a comfy recliner. I put my legs up and eyed the cup of cold coffee sitting on the table. There were three orange pills next to the coffee that he had arranged as the points of a triangle.

"Not if you don't take these," I said. I swept the pills into my hand and gave them to him. He took them, placed them on the floor, and continued to whittle.

"Those are to shut me up. Aren't you my advocate?"

He had the fourteen sticks. He stopped for a minute and sucked on the last of his cigarette.

I took out a pocket flashlight and beamed him with it. He quickened his head around. His face had reddened since the last time I saw him: inches of wormy capillaries had sprouted on his cheeks. He shielded his face and worded some cuss, his breath reaching me like a whiff of sour baby. "That's a hell of a thing to pull," he said. I turned off the light and leaned toward him. He whispered, "I can't even buy a pack of hot dogs because the markets can't acknowledge me. You know what it's like to have a shitload of money in an account under a name that used to belong to you, but you can't access it because that name has been rescinded?" He thumped the floor with one of the branches.

The Town Council had rescinded my client's identity for, as they claimed, "illegally changing the geography of our Homeland."

I leaned back and looked through the drapes. Across the street was one of the houses the Council claimed he "manipulated," having been deemed "outside of Council authority" and "outside of known physical laws."

Someone opened the drapes on the second floor. They were spying on us.

"You can get your name back if we can prove that you're..." I paused and took a drag of my cigarette. "...capable."

"I'm not gonna do it, goddamned it. They're not gonna have me reshape my last map. I just can't be a liar." He poured water from a cup into his eyes as if this would relieve the quarks of hurt. "I didn't change the geography, man." He shook his head. "I documented what was already there."

"Calm down," I said, lighting a smoke. "I'm not asking you to reshape, for Christ's sake. But you gotta appear... you know... somewhat reasonable in the proceedings." I motioned my head toward the orange pills on the floor. "It's medicine. And the right kind. Look, I'm here to help and I don't think the maps you've drawn... are bullshit. I mean, I've gone over this with you. But things take precedent. Like your eyes for God's sake. And these sticks?" I walked over to one and dabbed my fingertip over the sharp nub. "You're getting worse. It's not going to look good if they you're planning to poke out your eyes."

"I know what I'm doing," he said.

"Yeah, but why are you doing it?"

He stood up and backed away from me. For a minute, I thought he'd stab me right then. He opened his palm to the orange pills. "These little fuckers remind me of itsy-bitsy rotten teeth of this girl I knew in elementary school. God-awful Mercy with the hideous smile. Mercy Klein when she opened her mouth showed everyone her rotten, orange little pitiful teeth. Dumb Mercy of my elementary school." He tossed them onto the gutted couch near the window. "I just ask for my name to be unrescinded, a bit of justice. Every man needs his Jonathan."

"And I'm working on that, but it takes time.

Come here, sit down." He sat next to me and reeked of mulch. He put his hands on his lap.

"...if you were born without eyelids..." he said.

I came to explain the legal matter, but he stared off through the window to that other house across the way. The Town Council had covered the street signs with rags. They had erased all his footsteps. His address had been turned upside down to resemble some kind of dead language. Unfortunately, his most recent map came out in the year when some airborne salt had eroded the bodies of our vehicles and defaced our beloved wagons. They held his maps responsible for all the things that were going wrong. As I explained, my palm on his folded hands, I looked with him into that house across the way, seeing shapes in the window.

I could feel someone watching us.

"When you put your home and those other houses outside the established parameters of the municipality, it gave them a loophole to take away your identity. But if we can prove that you didn't do this with any malice, they'll designate your Christian name back to you, just like in Creation."

"You're saying that I caused this because I'm not right... that my map is insane?"

"It's just a legal maneuver."

He stood up and clutched one of the sharpened branches. "I should do it to you like the boar you are." He walked off and opened a closet in the hallway. He threw the stick in there and mumbled something under his breath like, "...and grandmamma killin' sects" or "...in my hand, Mama'll kill this six." I couldn't make it out. He went into the bathroom and groaned, pre-sumably sitting on the toilet. He was up to something.

The Council had discerned that he'd been responsible for the catastrophes in town because of the changes he had made on his newest map. I tried to argue that they were just coincidences. The last map preceded the salt-erosion of our pickups and cars, scaling through the bodies and leaving just husks and engines. Even the town's immaculate Fire Truck gave up during a call to placate some flames on the spot designated as the "New Civilization" on my client's map. We've been bugging ever since. Also, the brick had become nearly useless. Where he designated "The Epicenter of Things to Come," the Town had built a city wall out of the old fashioned materials: brick, mortar, and labor. The wall tumbled during a ritual procession of children celebrating the upward flow of rivers like the Nile, even spanking several child heads—them dying. They concluded it wasn't a physical problem of cement, but a conceptual one wherein the straight line was outmoded somehow, leaving place for the fall of this great object and all concrete eruditions to follow. My client's map had permanently damaged some of the perfect forms of things (e.g. the brick). They said it was too dangerous to proceed with any new construction projects. The old map had to be reinstated or the new one reshaped, they thought, and this would restore order.

And there was the heap of stillborns (four, I think) found on June 6 near the roots of our giant maple tree where he said a "New Forest" would appear.

My client asserted, of course, that he was simply documenting new geographies, and that any claim that he had caused any of the town's catastrophes was ludicrous.

I pounded on the bathroom door, ready to knock down the wall. It was as if this whole predicament was concocted so he could erect walls against me and others, he being the alone type. "Let me in. This isn't going to solve anything," I said, trying to conjure his old name. "This too shall pass, as the saying goes," I said. "It's just a matter of convincing them that it wasn't your fault, you know." I shifted my weight onto my bad foot. I had banged it that morning, somehow, simply putting on my shoe. The toenail would have to grow back. "I'm already talking to my salt expert friend who can explain the whole thing about our darned wagons going to shit. And I'm speaking to others about the other things. It's not you and I want you to know I know it's not you." I waited outside there like some kind of chided prostitute, foreseeing what's due me. He opened the door, handling that crappy belt of his. I could see he had been adding new holes to that leather because he'd been losing weight consistently for some time.

"They're wasting me," he said, handing me a handful of his own hair. It sat in my hand like a trilobite fossil: sprawled, black, and dead. All that hair made me want to wash my hands. "They sent you to collect this, I know it," he said.

I didn't know what he was talking about at the time. "Why would I want your hair?" I asked. I was dumbfounded and hungry at that point. During that period, I had come to suppress my hunger like a mediocre Machiavellian, thinking the ends justified the means, and wasting myself, realizing that the real catastrophe was that I had begun to repress all my drives.

"You don't think I see their spies watching me from across the street? They're making me waste away into nothingness simply by watching me."

I had a hand full of his dark curls, my toenail throbbing like a heart, and all I could think of was simmering stew of the worst kind. Back then, I would cram lukewarm gruel into my cheeks thinking that the next of many catastrophes would be a famine or drought or both, but I'd always end up rescinding my food even worse and couldn't pack away the energy (like the best of parasites can) for a later date. "Why would I want your hair?" I stared at the splotchy wallpaper. I thought maybe this wasn't wallpaper at all lining his home, but baptisms or something leaking through from a broken seam in a pipe.

"For the DNA, man. It's obvious they not only want to reshape the map, but they want to expunge me from history—to clone and make a new me—as if I had never existed. But this will not stop our town's erosion." He stood there, again adjusting his belt around his waist, and I couldn't encourage myself enough to look at him in the eye.

I lost that battle. I stared at his chest through the hoary yarn of his T-shirt. I had become afraid that I initially was wrong and that maybe he didn't have eyelids, but I knew that was a bit paranoid and attributed it to being famished. He said they had done it before. "Isn't that why they sent you, my Advocate?" he said.

I stuffed his hair into my pocket. "They wouldn't clone a man from hair alone," I said in passing. The crude peas and blotches on his wallpaper began to look like food. He stepped closer to me, almost breathing directly on my face. His expression was that of a lame dog hunkering down for strength. The under part of his eyes were bluish and cold from too much thinking, I supposed. But my stomach curdled. I cracked my knuckles and was looking around for one of those wooded sharps.

"And what else do they need?" he asked in a hoarse woman's whisper.

I backed away from him then, literally walking backward as he followed me until I reached behind me for the front door. Instead, I opened a closet. In it, I made out one of his maps that looked as if it had been etched on a pelt. The map was tacked to the back of the closet. In there, the house's pipes wove their way through as if the architects had not planned correctly for the flow of indoor plumbing, and they hung and elbowed through the greater area of the closet like the legs of a Mastiff. "Get out," he said, closing in on me, still adjusting his belt. I thought he might strangle me with the belt. As I sought the front door, I collided with the couch and found my way out onto the porch. I caught one last glimpse of him sitting on the floor, sharpening branches once again. It was that scrape-of-bone sound the whittling made.

On the eroding pavement in front of the house, there were mounds of ground stone or ash. They weren't large piles, but like anthills desolate among the small mass of street surface. I kicked a couple of mounds and looked up to the end of a pole where the street sign should have been. It was gone, but I thought I had seen a sign there earlier. I began to walk, but stopped as I was about to turn the corner and saw a man and a woman standing on the porch of the house my client and I had been staring at earlier. The man had his arm around the woman's shoulder, dressed in a cheap black suit. His pants were too short. She was outlined in a simple bridal uniform and had this look on her face of a dull winter. She opened her mouth almost right before some words blurted out incongruously, "Hello, next door."

I waved, still thinking I must put this behind me and grab at least some stale bread to sop up the stomach acid. I stood for a moment, but I couldn't put my finger on what was perturbing me about them. "I'm a neighbor," she said, still rolling her eyes as if she were an infant making out new shapes. "You're a neighbor?" She tapped the porch wood with her flat dress shoes as if this were part of the communication. The man, presumably her husband, held a scroll in his hand. "We're making neighbors," she mouthed. It looked more like she was a dubbed movie.

I knew, then, that they were from The Council.

"I'm visiting... kin," I said. I held my right hand to my belly like I had to vomit. I looked back to see if my client had come out of his house, but his front door was as shut as ever. I noticed that the side of his house had begun to chip away to an older layer of paint—a mushroom flavor.

"Making neighbors," she said. They choreo-graphed their descent down from the front steps awkwardly, almost tripping. They landed on the pavement just across from me. She continued to plunder the air above her with her eyes.

I stood. I knew that I should've run. Instead, I cleared my throat. "You all just get married?" I asked.

They shook their heads. "There is no one but me to matrimony and I cannot matrimony myself," she said. "I'm not a matrimony, however I look..." It was obvious she was lip-syncing and it was the man who was speaking. She continued with her lip imitations, but it was him I focused on as he read from the scroll as if it were a script.

I began to panic and played upon his crotch with my own eyes. I then turned around and saw my client in his window, staring at this couple and me. Their wordings continued as I tried to sign something to him inconspicuously with my hands down around my hips like, *These are them*, but he didn't pick up on me doing this. His new neighbors must have been investigators or spies, I had concluded. I got caught up with trying to warn him that these were probably them and we were then in our last leg of the proceed-ings—that this conversation, was, in fact, part of The Trial. My client had the knife near his chest, whittling those branches like he had no other nervous tick to confide in. But the couple was saying, "Please... please... return the paraphrase."

"Excuse me?"

The man, eyeing me through glasses as thick as a manhole cover, handed me the scroll of paper. On it was our whole conversation written out in courier as if this conversation had been scripted long before. There were descriptions of our gestures, almost accurate illustrations of that day's weather and shade, so I skipped down to where I was supposed to respond. I didn't bother looking at what they had said (since I had missed it trying to warn my client), and simply read in the most monotone imitation of my own voice, "Excuse me? I... don't... understand."

I handed the scroll back to the man, who swiped it away from me and whined out the woman's part. Her lip-quivering and miming had become lamer, colder, insincere. She had been lip-syncing his voice. "As I was saying, since we are neighboring, you will please rescind our neighbor's hair and birth certificate?"

The man passed the script back to me, and I had the idea of eating the damn scroll. I cleared my throat and I likened my voice to the child actor I once pictured myself as, and read aloud, "But will this be enough? But will we not need more DNA? But will he not do the same thing once he is reinvented? But will not the map designate the catastrophes once again?" I knew this wasn't anything I would've said because I'm not as stilted and retarded as this, but I knew I had to go along. I looked back to my client in his window, but his drapes were closed and there was no light in there whatsoever. I turned back to the woman. She continued to graze the upper thunder with her eyes (the climate itself going a bit fucked) as if to read the clouds for snow or hieroglyphs.

"Go with the hair," the man whined, his arm still lying on top of the woman's shoulders. She mouthed it, but I could've sworn she did it poorly and even worse than before. I think she mouthed, *Get out. Save yourself.* Perhaps she had been mouthing this warning all along.

***

I entered my client's home the next day, again getting lost on the way there and ending up at first on a path that led to our giant maple tree, but finally made it. He was gone. Someone had restored a bit of order back to the cartographer's living space, though. He stood great with a top hat and cane (a photograph of himself and a man that looked a bit like him at a ball celebrating the achievements of dead mayors), framed on his wall, and with a great smile. The picture was autographed, *Philosopher of Calamity!* That was a big joke.

On a piece of scratch paper were some of the etchings of his newest map. "I have observed that at least three homes will be the epicenter of disaster," he had written. "It is there I have discovered the undoing of physics." There was a bloody fingerprint in the margin. "In impossibility," he wrote, "I have discovered animate meat... humans *a priori.*"

On another crumpled piece of paper, in penmanship that looked like pubic hair, was part of the conversation I had with his neighbors.

I shivered and nearly hacked up a lung.

I began to gather as much hair as I could: from brushes, in between seat cushions, on top of his greasy pillow, etc. I was also told to gather fingernails.

There's nothing I fear more in this world than hair and fingernails.

I was to gather bills, opened and unopened, from the floor and put them in specially marked plastic containers. Throw any uneaten food from the fridge into Wednesday night's garbage (particularly leftovers, like the curdled ham that was in there making the place peculiar). Get rid of eyeglasses. Just throw them in a heap somewhere. (There were three hundred forty-nine horn-rimmed glasses—one without lenses—that I eventually put next to that giant maple tree—and eleven prescriptions for others). Put clothes in a pile next to the neighbor's leaves and burn them to cinders. Save, please save, his birth certificate (and anything with his name on it). Leave the maps there. Again, just leave them. (I came across three bottles of orange pills and thought of taking one. The label warned, *Will Make You Sleep*.)

But his diary, I kept for myself. They didn't mention it, so I just put the thing under my coat and walked away with it. There were three entries, each strangely enough, in different penmanship, as if he had written them using different hands each time, but that would only account for two:

"I will be known."

"They will not give me back my name."

"Fourteen months after I write this, the town will be entirely buried in ash."

I don't know when he made this proclamation.

THE HELTER-SKELTER WAR

The far post in the damselfly bog is deadly. "Like staring at the sun," people say. The laborers that harvest the muck—eighth-generation progenies of Chinese labor with resplendent, ruby-colored eyes—are shackled together at the ankle. They speak in a mixture of teeth-chatters and whispers. It's something they do with their grip of the earth and dance rituals that spawns new damselflies. They crease their webbed fingers through mud, handling fistfuls, spitting into their palms every so often. The laborers wear linen and ashen faces.

Walter M., a gun-runner and weapons developer, doesn't allow the workers to wear gloves. This would inhibit chemistry between hand oils and earth. Mugginess lasts for a lifetime at this job. Every noon, a sputtering propeller airplane mists them. The men look up, eyes closed, and open their palms upward. The far post sticks out of the bog like a spine. It's a marker for something horrifying.

Walter M. scratches himself while standing behind the screen door. He thinks no one can see him. He has a screwy eye that leaks. He pours a cup of tea into his slit of a mouth and counts heads. Twenty-four workers. No one missing. No added mishaps. He empties the last of a bottle of tranquilizers into his gullet. He abhors the sunlight. The hum of a tractor's engine lulls somewhere on the horizon. Not far from here, farmers grow wheat and corn. But Walter M. knows that food is something from the past. He believes that there needs to be new food products—new animals—as weapons. He chugs another cup of tea and steps outside.

Crunching, clobbering, and the mulchy slap of

workers' hands against mud. Damp earth squishes through fingers—hence, the genius. That sound could be music if it weren't so terrible. Standing over his men, Walter M. hurries a finger into his nose: his thinking posture. In the past, he would have shouted or killed one or two just to show the rest what's up. *Listen, fuckers, I know couple of you is leaking information.* He says nothing. Yesterday, the popping sound of growing eggs began. It's incessant. Near crazy-making. The laborers sense Walter's heated tongue. His verbs. They don't sing and there's no reverie. It's rumored that he ate a man once. A small, stupid guy, sure. But a man nonetheless.

"Keep muddling," he says to one of the workers. "Keep whoring the bog ground. God's working through your fingernails."

That's the secret. They say the workers have been bred for the special lubricants in their hands. Walter M. plops down on a beach chair. He picks up a day-old newspaper. He had tucked his will inside of it. He scans the will, wiping away grease from his eye with his finger, and daydreams. He would leave most of his assets—his iron bed where he had thought of weapons to destroy God, dog-eared books, a telescope, and the bundles of money buried in coffins near the bog—to people who are already dead. He breathes heavily. It's simply one more hot, scurvy-like day of the WAR. He stands up. He puts a twenty-year old toothpick into his mouth and smiles. "I've run a factory for weapons, but I never ran a bog," he says to himself. This seems funny to him. Two workers turn around and glance at him.

"Your muddling is good, boys!" The popping sound is like locusts. "This thing will kill every one of them," he mutters. He eyes a red tractor in the heat-glimmers across the way.

***

Jeb, a mid-level COMBAT ANALYST for the DEPARTMENT OF WAR-PRACTICE OVERSIGHT, is safe inside his bunker. He stays there for weeks at a time. The air is stuffy like night-sheets. He sits cross-legged on a rug while ignoring the hurt inside his stomach. His suit smells like soot. He concentrates on the steel walls. There are thousands of seams and bolts demarcating each section of steel. For every bolt, there are dozens of citizens, some dead or with amputations. CIVIL WAR II has been outlandish compared to THE FIRST in 1861. Jeb is sorry that he hasn't been able to mitigate the horrors, but he can't remember an epoch without smoke and teeth in the air. He travels throughout the country via catacombs, visiting underground homes for OFFICERS and other ANALYSTS. He is voracious and his favorite meal is a stack of pancakes with sticky jam and a glass of milk with a dollop of whiskey. He never imagined himself a military man, but he grew to savor the gallop of fire and explosions.

Jeb's duty is to surreptitiously analyze battle scenes: the means of death, the wounds, number of limbs crushed or exploded, the disbursement of bodies, etc., particularly those of civilians. On the surface, his duty is to minimize damage.

The DEPARTMENT OF WAR-PRACTICE OVERSIGHT—with its origin in the CONGRESSIONAL BUDGET OFFICE—is an unbiased, non-partisan enforcer of CIVIL WAR II's established RULES OF ENGAGEMENT.

During his tenure, Jeb has recommended abolishing the names of weapons responsible for the greatest number of casualties.

He even recommended the abolishment of the names of diseases.

He and his staff theorized that if they outlawed labels, the objects themselves would disappear.

They outlawed the name for the mechanism-with-a-handle-that-shoots-cone-shaped-steel.

For several weeks afterward, there were only

knifings and strangulations. Then busted-up heads returned. Holes in faces and bodies became regular again with red caves in cheeks and skulls full of splinters—but where did the wounds come from? The name of the weapon disappeared, but the consequences resurfaced, although haphazardly at first. The origin of the wounds—whether revolver or semi-automatic—no longer had a NOUN. The DEPARTMENT OF WAR-PRACTICE OVERSIGHT theorized that after the weapon's name was "archived," the combatants' memories of the mechanism would dissolve into blurry, indefinable objects.

WAR has a funny way of mining the unconscious for any means of annihilation.

Men had to practice reusing the indefinable tool. It is now known the shape of the mechanism is genetically imprinted upon HUMAN CONSCIOUSNESS, much like an infant recognizes his mother's face without having met her, without knowing her name, and without having learned to love her. The shapes of things are sometimes simply *there*.

After a battle, Jeb scours the scene with his computer and creates a glossary of the most likely means of death.

He spends weeks documenting each mode of death to better ascertain which SIGNIFIERS to ban and slow down the slaughter.

But Jeb's secret obsession is his MUSEUM OF EYES. He has a taste for shape, volume, density, color, and *intention*. He prefers the eyes of the living, but has nearly free reign of the dead. He perfected a spoon with a beveled razor on one of its sides to scoop out the eyes whole.

He stores the eyes in airtight aquariums in a vault to which only he has the key—each specimen labeled, codified, and coated with a special lacquer.

Cluster bombs and shrieking soothe Jeb's mind, even from inside his bunker.

This is a WAR without governments. The CONGRESSIONAL, JUDICIAL, AND EXECUTIVE BRANCHES have turned a blind eye. The TWO WARRING FACTIONS are fighting for their respective *living aesthetics*.

FACTION A, having originated one hundred miles outside of New Orleans, believes in a NEW ETIQUETTE: the man-wig; sign-language instead of verbal speech; mandated meditation; genderless garb; semi-automatics with bayonets for all men; and that HUMAN CONSCIOUSNESS is the proverbial *ghost in all machines*.

FACTION B, having originated north of Albuquerque, demands a RETURN TO BASENESS: madness as guru; see-through clothing; no-more-shaving; a private police force that mandates sodomy as *the coming-of-age experience*; the end of antibiotics; and that brains simply broadcast *thoughts that have always existed*.

Jeb looks into the mirror hanging on the wall of his bunker.

He is a light-skinned, biracial man.

He has straightened reddish hair, glowing lime-colored eyes, and a deeply neutral expression.

Jeb considers himself a connoisseur of *seeing*.

***

Darkness sinks over the bog as Walter M. flashes the far post with a flashlight. He begins feeding the bog: cornhusks, old shirts, and a small motor. He unpacks a dirty lunch bag and sniffs the white brick of powder inside. He sticks his toothpick into the bag and tastes it. He is feeding the bog cocaine. He slaps it on thick over the skin of the water. The powder clumps at first, and then sinks. Walter M. grasps his mechanism-with-a-handle-that-shoots-cone-shaped-steel, stirs the juices like some home-brewed concoction, and pierces the surface with a rusty bayonet. He wipes the blade of the bayonet with his finger and licks it. Nothing really comes up from the bog—few air bubbles and sick gas, but not more than usual. The mosquitoes here are as large as pigs. He swats the mosquitoes and imagines gummy, burgeoning arms deep inside the bog mucking up the earth, cocaine, slime-fuck, and the dead. Walter M. leans on his antique mechanism-with-a-handle-that-shoots-cone-shaped-steel and spits into the bog. He lights the far post again with his flashlight and sees capsule-sized eggs budding on it.

He will go to sleep on his iron bed for a week, envisioning himself as some kind of Edison. The fact is, he simply invents weapons. Upon reaching his cottage just a few dozen yards away, he cracks open his front door and jumps onto his stitched-up, soiled mattress.

***

The AMERICAN RUBYSPOT damselfly births at night.

The laborers sleep near the bog's bank, culling leaves and twigs as pillows. Each laborer is a piano key in a line of sleepers.

The sunlight will bleed damselfly bodies spectacularly red. *Two spherical penetrating eyes.*

Like the fleshy seeds of a pomegranate.

The new weapon.

Winged. Opaque and veined and spidery.

Their shapes will disappear into the shade.

RUBYSPOTS feed on soft-bodied insects.

But these engineered damselflies subsist on *thoughts*. And the laborers dream of each other.

RUBYSPOTS, of nearly ten thousand replications, at first feed on the laborers' sleep resins—near the crust of their eyes, and on the periphery of the men's haws.

Two of the laborers cough. One of their webbed hands compresses the earth.

Thousands of naiads climb the stem of the plants from which they came, into the sky and into THE LIFE.

***

A week later, Walter M. sleeps with his hand on his crotch. It's morning. He dreams of Big Wind, the three-hundred pound girth of woman who pounced on his love in New Orleans. In the dream, it's the turn of the millennium. A brothel: tobacco smoking, pool, and moonshine in the saloon downstairs. Upstairs, Big Wind lies on two queen beds squished together. She has half a country for tits, a face more beautiful than his mama, two able hands, and thighs that would high-jack rich men across the globe.

"Walter M., get your ugly white ass over here," she stammers through her drunk teeth. She wears a slinky night thing, frilly materials around the vagina, but mostly a smell of gauzed-up sex. Walter M. has a question mark in this dream. *Why do I have a boner for the deeply confused?*

"You're a blur," Walter M. says.

She unleashes one of her titan breasts. "Got your gravity right here, sugar." She shakes it and shakes heaven. "Get your peter."

Walter M. is aroused and half-awake. *Do bosses have wet dreams?* But then he sprouts upward out of his mucky bed. "They're mashing the mud already!" he yelps while looking out his window.

The Chinese-descendent laborers mouth cusses as they squish the mud through their webbed fingers. Thousands of AMERICAN RUBYSPOTS swirl around and around the bog.

Walter M. knows the damselflies' redness will be the scourge of the earth.

There is a slight wetness on his crotch.

The bog scum sweats onto his window screen. The panes are open. The morning hums. It's God-forsaken summer all year.

Walter M. plops back down on his bed because he's remorseful for his teenage years. There had been scores of dumbass decisions. He hates the military, hates FACTION A and FACTION B, and even hates the South. He wrinkles up his acne and closes his eyes. "I am a sad man." As a kid, he dreamed of being a cardiovascular surgeon. He used to visualize big-breasted women cooing as he sewed up the chest of an important general. But he ended up a technician of damselfly terror. He turns bog scum into DEATH. He is a TERRORIST.

He hears fire-fighting erupt, the bloodletting and our God sponging up the rot with his tongue. DEATH shrieks. Walter M. hears the boots of thousands of disillusioned combatants pound against swamp ground.

"Murder all of them motherfuckers," he mutters.

Walter M. will summon all the AMERICAN RUBYSPOT damselflies against the faceless hordes.

***

That night, RUBYSPOTS trek through the Southern front toward the combatants and swirl deadly in the space around their dreaming heads. Walter M. wears the necessary earplugs. It's the fluttering of the RUBYSPOTS' wicked wings that make all combatants deranged.

The sound of RUBYSPOTS seeps into combatants' brains as the men murder and maim. One combatant, a bit of an idiot savant, pictures a house with skin-draped wings wedging its way into his head as he dies.

Combatants' brains were never meant to house such evil sounds.

It's a long, deadly morning. There are battles. Blood goes every which way. One combatant has his face eaten off by an alligator. But mostly, steel rips up these boys. It's WAR. A FACTION B platoon gathers around the perimeter, trying to squeeze out the crackers from their holed-up hiding places. Even if the mechanism-with-a-handle-that-shoots-cone-shaped-steel lost its name, WAR presses on.

A black man is eating another combatant's foot. The combatant, race unknown, simply gapes as if attempting to laugh.

Some university boy masturbates in the swamp for no good reason at all. "Shit, the war mongers!" he screams as he's beheaded.

There are thousands of them. Men.

Even a couple hundred spears land from outer space.

There are corpses and there are hours. There are heaps of meat, a jaw, several hundred orphaned arms, legs unidentified, a heart in a tree, kidneys even ruined for dialysis, a wishbone, ribs good for the harp, an angel-shaped skin slough, gourds, the fish smell, and the deadly whizzing of the damselflies.

The combatants are eating each other.

One guy, a lieutenant from FACTION A, turns to a Chinese laborer and says, "You have to shoot me in the head! I'm fucking dead already! I saw it in a movie!"

Twenty combatants creep up the hill—some carrying the shooting-mechanism backward-aimed. Damselflies gossip around their heads and daydreams. One on the far right asks, "What are we doing here again?"

Two grenades go off. Several are decimated and the others don't know what to make of their colleagues except to guffaw and applaud.

A man with his teeth missing screams out, "Fuck all this! I brought a pick axe!"

A damselfly latches onto the back of his head. The combatant plows up the hill, yelling, "I'm gonna get you, whoever you are!"

At the top of the hill, a diamond-edged saw-blade splits him in half.

Jeb is about thirty yards away gathering RUBY-

SPOTS with a net. Jeb wears a well-pressed suit, a bulletproof vest and earplugs for protection. He rips the wings off one of the RUBYSPOTS and speaks into his walkie-talkie. "These dragonflies are everywhere. They seem to distort the RULES OF ENGAGEMENT... Yes, sir... I'll need to find the name for them, send it to the TAXONOMY BOARD." Jeb puts the walkie-talkie away and swats some of the damselflies away from his face. He's disappointed at failing to minimize the damage of WAR.

Near the top of a hill, Jeb kneels near a half-Irish soldier. "Some water?" Jeb asks, offering his canteen. He makes sure not to muddy his suit pants.

The combatant has one violet eye. He has a jagged slash in his chest. The hole makes a wet balloon sound when he weeps.

"That like moonshine?" the combatant whimpers.

"It's like LIFE," Jeb says.

Jeb shakes a dribble into the combatant's maw.

"How?"

"Excuse me?" Jeb asks. He pushes his thick glasses back onto his nose. "I don't understand."

"Don't got any potato liquor?"

"I only have water." Jeb stands and pulls up his suit pants near his navel.

"What's all that commotion I'm thinking?" the man asks.

Jeb sighs and takes a swig from his canteen. "What a horrible smell out here, huh?" He starts to pace as smoke rises from the dark, red-steeped hill. "We tried to rescind usages, parts of the grammar of weapons, NOUNS, even reexamined the meaning of *sharpness*, but you think that stopped the mayhem?"

"You run this place or just work here?" the combatant asks.

Jeb shakes his head and sits back down. He can't keep from staring at the man's violet eye. Jeb sips water and shakes some more into the dying man's mouth. He squishes three ants in the grass. "WAR makes me ravenous," Jeb exclaims.

The combatant tries to lift his heavy head. "I don't know nothing about any war."

Jeb massages his tongue with his finger. "I have this terrible taste in my mouth."

"Lick something... last night?" The combatant's voice is giving out.

"No. I'm just very, very hungry." Jeb gulps down more water. "Jesus... just can't get enough of this water."

"Sure is good," the combatant says. He looks sorry-eyed and drunk. "Where can I get some of this stuff?"

A refinery looms like a bad tooth on the horizon.

"Where you from anyway, soldier?"

"Originally from New Orleans." The man is bleeding to death.

"I sexed many a prostitute in that city," Jeb exclaims, his hands in his pockets, and stares out over the hill.

A damselfly buzzes around Jeb's head.

"Did your mother have gorgeous eyes?" Jeb asks.

The combatant coughs up blood. "Yeah, my mama was pretty. She had pretty eyes, I suppose."

"Eyes are like a fine scotch, my friend. You've got some wondrous globes."

"Thank you, sir," the combatant says and dies.

***

Walter M. drunk-walks up the bloodied hill. He wears a grin as his brief period of guilt passes. He escalated each FACTION's murderous capacity, but now he's got a belly full of potato liquor and a head full of fucking. Can't get the Big Wind out of his mind. He shakes his head and laughs as he steps over a whimpering combatant.

Once at the top of the hill, he notices the Chinese laborers gathered together in a circle in the valley.

After strolling through wrecked corpses for an hour, Walter M. comes upon a light-skinned black man in a suit and bulletproof vest. How goddamned weird, he thinks. "Hello, sir," Walter M. ventures. "Are you an officer of one of the FACTIONS?"

Jeb turns his attention toward Walter M. "Not exactly."

"Jesus, Mary, and Joseph," Walter M. says after lighting a smoke. He sits next to Jeb, overlooking the heaps of meat. "All this is useless, isn't it?" He takes a deep, deep drag. "Had my one true girth-of-love in my mind throughout this satanic shit."

Jeb tenses his back and examines an AMERICAN RUBYSPOT damselfly for a long moment. The RUBYSPOT lands on a twig. It's extraterrestrial. Red as sundown. Two bloodshot, globular eyes.

An earplug had fallen out of Jeb's ear.

"Hear that?" Jeb asks.

"This fat girl, Big Wind, was the love of my cheap life. I would've married her. I would've lived inside her." Walter M. turns toward Jeb. "Got a girl?" He repositions himself and plops his right hand on a man's calf in the grass.

Jeb is succumbing to the AMERICAN RUBYSPOT's hypnotic fluttering. "I just had a vision of a vampire right now... somebody who'd murder us all... did you see him?"

"I dunno if you're crazy or dreaming or not. Why you asking me? We're all dreaming for all I know." Walter M. smiles, sucks a lovely drag on the cig as he prides himself on his unique, damselfly terrorism.

"Shit," Jeb says. "Yeah, I have an obese lover,

too."

"What color eyes she got?" Walter M. observes ten, maybe fifteen, damselflies swarming around them. It's almost as if they're teasing.

"Not sure," Jeb says. He panics and his heart swells because he has never felt the obviousness of impending doom. "Shit, who the hell is that down there?"

One of the laborers gallops up the hill toward them atop a muscled, black horse.

Jeb observes an opaque and massive wing jutting from under the laborer's shirt. "It's a Chinese fucking vampire!"

Walter M. fantasizes about his former lover, Big Wind, and sighs. "It's just one of my boys."

From atop his muscled horse, the laborer looms over them—unscathed by the RUBYSPOTS' deadly fluttering—and unveils a titanium sword from its scabbard. He mumbles through chapped lips, "You're both fucking done."

GRIEF!

I stub my toe on a woman. She's spread out next to the tub. Her breasts rise and fall. I reach down and rub the hair on her legs. There's a skirt over her important areas. She's got a face like a sprain. If she wakes up, I believe I can help her. I'm not a bad man. The poor girl. She's got lipstick all over her face. Her mascara has smeared and those eyes keep going back and forth. I've got to shave, but I step backward instead and leave the bathroom door open in case she awakens terrorized or dies.

Through my window overlooking the street, I watch the drones in their burlap suits hurl rubbish into the garbage truck. One of them pulls a lever and the mechanical mouth crunches bags. It's as if the drones have faces made of cake and glue. They all wear the same bloated expression and heat comes off their tongues. It's basically dark out, the beginning of morning, and I try to focus on their meaty hands. They grasp so many and so much.

The garbage truck steams away.

The woman staggers into my living room. "I can't find my bed," she mutters. She rubs her face, smearing lipstick onto her cheeks. She plops down on the couch and takes a sip of cold coffee from a cup sitting on the table. "It's the end of the world if I can't find it."

I remember that I had encountered her in my bathroom.

"Did I wake you up out of some nightmare?"

"Don't interrupt me," she says sharply. She rubs her already messy hair. "You always interrupt me."

Her face is blotchy. She says nothing. I smoke two cigarettes and imagine her holding my baby,

35

rocking the child in her arms. I am next to her. I actually picture myself: skin straight out of summer, a brawny chest without hair, and a navel that does not look like my own. There are three possibilities:

1. She's my wife.
2. She's a stranger.
3. She's not human.

"Have you ever lost your bed before?" I ask.

She looks up at me and there is terror in her pupils as if she has crawled out from a fissure in the air.

"I haven't lost it *per se*," she says. Somehow, I feel as if this isn't her natural tone of voice. She lifts her skirt just above her knees and I have a flash of anger. My face reddens and I begin to railroad cuss through my brain. I focus on her kneecaps.

"You said I always interrupt you?" I am aware of an itch roaming through my body. I focus on my neck, throat, chest, and then stomach, all of which become hot. "That means we know each other."

She fishes through her purse.

"Of course!" she screams. "I'm your wife." She gives me this coy look while holding a condom.

I can hear the garbage truck making its rounds somewhere down the block.

"Oh shit," I say under my breath, looking at the condom. "The mechanism."

She saunters toward me. Her eyes are like small, deep-sea prey. How gorgeous and strangely green! She pulls her skirt up a bit further. "Machinations," she whispers. Her thighs are muscular.

I begin to shake.

"Don't pout, puppy dog. Don't you want to *be* me?" She has unzipped herself by this point. She wears lacy undergarments and a smell that would drive most canines frenzied.

"I don't know you."

"Don't play shy." She's jigging her plump bottom in front of my mouth.

"I'm an historian for God's sake!" I yell.

"That job has got you tame," she throats. "Always searching for meaning." She strips to her nakedness. "Don't forget who you *are*, now."

"And what's that?"

I had come to show very little affection for my wife. I was aroused only when I pretended she was a stranger. In the beginning of our relationship, it was different. She would often have her hair in a bun. She wore oversized clothes around the house. She was soap-like, clean. I can say that her breath was humid. We met in college. (She once said she had spotted me from several yards away and thought we would have smart, bigheaded children.)

Her face was an illumination.

She had asked me to meet her at her apartment after I finished class. She seduced *me*. "Come on," she said. She summoned me with her finger. She licked her very white teeth. She was a shape in the doorframe. There were thirteen steps to her front door. She looked at the ground, but I know she meant to lure me. I picked up my leaden feet. *Clunk, clunk!* like Franken-stein. "Come on..." I was a goof. My jacket was too big, a terrible shade of green. Her hair was wet and she wore a robe and sandals. Muffin, her cat with a missing right eye, rubbed against her legs and meowed. "Come in," she whispered as I reached the top of the steps. She placed her palm on my unshaven face. *Sheeeiiit*, I thought. She must have been talking to me. I was peeking into her home (e.g., vacuum cleaner still plugged in, a pile of books in the hallway, bed without a frame, waft of lemon furniture polish). Her palm arrived at my lips. Was I supposed to kiss her fingers?

She grabbed my arm and was nibbling on my ear.

I stared at the orifice in the cat's face where his

eye should have been.

"That's Muffin," she said.

I could see gigantic areolas under her robe.

"Those are large," I said.

"God, you taste good."

We kissed sloppily. I unbuttoned my jacket, threw it on the bed and almost tripped. Muffin followed us, purring.

"I've wanted you ever since Revolutions of the Twentieth Century." She stuck her tongue in my mouth for a bit, and then paused. "When you stood up in class and said, 'Lenin's centralization of the Party led *directly* to opportunism, Stalinism, totalitarianism, and 20 million dead!' I mean, wow!" She grabbed my crotch.

"I would amend that," I said.

That's when I noticed the shelf. On it was a row of dildos and a .357 Magnum. "Jesus, Laconia, crucify me!" I screamed.

"Yes!" She disrobed. "Do you think you can satisfy me? Do you think you have what it takes?" Her breasts jousted.

I eased backward across the bed. She crept on top of me and grabbed and flipped me over. She was a big girl. Off with everything! I had no choice. The room smelled and I think I was happy. She grinned from ear to ear, showing off her *perfect* teeth. "Oh!" was the chorus of our matrimony. Muffin climbed on my back for a great ride while Laconia and I made love. The cat dug its needle-sharp nails into me. "Goddamned!" I screamed at the cat. "I'll fuck your eye!"

"Yes!"

Four months later, we got an apartment together.

I don't mean to misrepresent her. Sometimes, we play this game. I pretend to have discovered Calculus and the bending-by-stars around our bodies. "Venus gets to 900 degrees Fahrenheit," I tell her. This pretension of genius: my hand rubbing against her inner thigh bringing her to moan. She said she always wanted to marry a genius. All I need to do is stroke her or raise my fist at her and she emits a smell akin to vinegar. It isn't vulgar, but what is that burning-off smell? Now having postulated that I love her, she caresses my bottom and reaches out with her eyes. The way one does this is subtle. Do the pupils dilate? Do the eyes bulge? She would have me *be* her. "Venus indeed..." she utters as we cum. "Wife," she says a moment later.

"OK." I reach for my cigarettes. "Would you like a cigarette, dear?" It's the proper etiquette after sex. Smoke escapes into the ceiling.

"Laconia," she says.

"Where is she?"

"*My* name is Laconia."

If I were to characterize things before Laconia disappeared, I would have said things were peachy. We sat almost motionless in bed most days. "Please, kill me," she whispered in her sleep. In hindsight, I would have paid more attention to the little things: hairballs the size of tumbleweed, balled-up underwear near the bed, algae in the shower, etc. Not even coffee aroused her out of her stupor. We started to watch television much too often. She loved aliens and claimed to have had an extraterrestrial daughter. I dragged in a stationary bicycle from the sidewalk. The rusty bike's seat was chewed. I pedaled while she tried to sleep. The bike made a despicable ratcheting sound. As I cycled in the nude, she would lie on her back, her mouth half-open. My textbooks began to collect dust and cat hair. Sometimes, Muffin swiped at my legs as I rode the bike. I thought of smashing her. It would have been fun to smash her.

"Don't do it," I heard Laconia say.

Sirens whirled southward like a sound pool. Somewhere, a person was in trouble.

It's afternoon. That woman who claims to be my wife lies in my bed under the covers. She does not move. I face the mirror, part my hair on the side. I sweep the crust from my eyes. I'm dressed in a pinstriped suit that I wore to my high school graduation. I grab the flyers I made the day before. I chose my favorite photograph of Laconia for the flyer. It's centered under her name and the heading, *Missing*.

I stand in line like a soldier, waiting for my coffee. The coffee clerk's eyes are two bloodied eggs. How I've grown to hate him. I drink coffee with a furor. I don't like sugar, milk, creamer, honey, vanilla, or whiskey. Caffeine by itself goes straight to my dopamine house. The clerk stares at me. I don't know what he wants. My hands shake and I look over my shoulder. The fat woman from my apartment building (the woman who put a litter of dead kittens in the trash one time) is behind me. "Leland," I think I hear her say. "Are you still looking for your wife?" The clerk sneers. I could have sworn the fat woman said, "Laconia's not in zone 10025," and, "She's dead."

I try to stare straight ahead, but my legs begin to wobble. Finally, the clerk hands me my coffee. "Have a good day," he says. I turn to walk out.

The fat woman wipes her porky hands on her face. I smile because I'm polite. As I pass her on my way out, I whisper, "I know who you're hiding in your bedroom."

The fat woman frowns.

I walk the streets and post flyers of Laconia. This is what I do. Her face is plastered next to ads for moving trucks, etc. I have never gotten used to this city. I moved here on a whim with four packs of cigarettes and a hundred dollars. How many bricks are there in this city? I bum a cigarette from a teenage girl and rip off the filter. Night approaches. Lights appear like fireflies in a blackening sea. People rush by as cars do their quick rounds. There are horns, voices, clanging, steam, screeches, and a song even. Cars again, and I think it's the same half dozen clunkers over and over, perhaps with different drivers.

I must have been walking in circles.

A poster of my wife is glued on an overhang.

Naturally, I stop.

Who should I call?

Aliens must've abducted the wife.

Did I ever report her missing?

Is that really her? I thought she had hazel eyes?

Was she Jewish?

I think I hear my name floating through a crowd. "Beat it, buddy," some guy says trying to get past me.

"I lost my wife," I say.

He looks at me. "Be grateful," he says.

I lower my head.

I find myself downtown. I fold a flyer of my missing wife and put it in my wallet. There's a pair of binoculars on a bench.

"Hello, son," a woman says as I'm looking through the binoculars from the wrong end.

"Mom? I thought you were dead?" I turn around. It's only a nun.

"Can I sit with you?" she asks.

"I'm not sitting."

"What are you doing?"

"Looking through binoculars from the wrong end. It's not illegal, I swear."

"May I look?"

"I'm afraid not, sister. This is a job for professionals. When you look through the wrong end of binoculars, you don't see close-ups. You see the insides of people. It's horrible. That pregnant woman over there actually has a stomach full of quarters." I point.

The nun begins puffing on a pipe.

"Are you from that funeral party over there?" I ask.

She lets out a sphere of sweet pipe smoke. "Do you think the universe has a memory?"

"I lost my wife," I say. "I don't remember much of anything."

I sit next to the nun on the bench. She puts her chapped hand on my cheek. "There's a place where *all* of history is recorded.

"65 million years ago," she continues, "an asteroid killed the dinosaurs. We took over. But it's all here. A gang of asteroids and comets swing in ellipses around our sun. They *will* strike again." She folds her hands on her lap. "Do you have children?" she asks.

"No." I open my wallet and show her a photograph of Laconia.

"I like the sheep skin covers on the couch," she says. The nun's hands are dry as ash. "Who's the beautiful girl?"

"That's Laconia. I may know her and she is missing, I'm told."

"Did she kill herself?"

I snatch the photograph from the nun's hands.

She puts her hand on my thigh. Laconia would've been amused. "She's so young and beautiful," the nun says.

Stomach acid leaps against my ribs.

"What happened?" the nun asks again. "To her? To you?"

I begin to mouth an answer as if I were trying to pin down a fading dream. "I feel like I should know," I say.

Her attention suddenly turns toward the black sky. "I think it's the comets," the nun says.

"What is?" I place the photograph in my wallet next to my expired driver's license.

"Comets are balls of heavenly ice. Their molecules record every event that has ever happened. They can tell you everything."

I walk away.

She sits on the bench in the dark with her head down.

As I open the front door, I hear the television. The apartment's filled with a blue glow. It smells sickeningly sweet. Bed sheets lie in a ball in the hallway. I step over them. The woman is watching the news and sits on the couch wrapped in a blanket. I turn on a light and she whips her head around. Below her nose and eyes is a patch of dried blood. "Turn off the light, please," she says. I turn it off and plop down next to her.

She grabs my hand and massages it.

"The Drake Observatory reported that an asteroid came within 200,000 miles of hitting the earth," an anchorman reports.

"How are you?" she asks.

I force a yawn. "I'm fine, just a bit tired."

We sit in silence and watch the news for a few minutes.

"I wish you wouldn't spend all day away from me," she says and wraps the blanket around her body.

"I spent all day looking for you. You're either missing or you're dead."

Her thumb and forefinger dig into my palm.

"I was all over the place," I say.

"I dreamed about you," she says, rocking back and forth. "I miss you, Leland. I miss you so much."

"Yeah," I say.

I can't bear to have another wife, I think.

I find myself at the end of a cigarette I don't remember lighting. The room feels like a capsule in orbit. My stomach flutters and I'm lightheaded.

You're gonna end up marrying a whore, I recall my father saying to me. I was about eleven years old. He handed me a used Swiss Army knife because it was my birthday. His wife stormed in from the kitchen. She was scraping her red, raw hands. *You can't give him a knife*, she said. *What if he murders somebody?*

"I never meant to hurt you," I mutter through bubbles of saliva. I must be crying. "You gotta believe me."

"Stop it," Laconia says. "There's no use feeling guilty."

The glow of the television traces the outline of her body. She stands up and leads me by the wrist into our bedroom. We lie on the bare mattress holding hands and stare at the ceiling.

"I loved you deeply," I whisper into Laconia's ear.

On the street, a garbage drone heaps rubbish into his truck as the mechanical mouth bites down on it all, nearly to the bone.

"Of course you did," my wife says.

GOLDMINE, 1893

I was just a boy then. My hair went caboodle with a bed of cowlicks that my mother tried to suppress. I was probably eight, or maybe I was nine. My walk was clumsy, my two legs like bed springs, my arms skinny as needles and everything else about me, except my face, screamed out "amateur midget." I had a model's face. I would later think of this part of my life when I couldn't sleep. I've had many nights of insomnia. At eight or maybe nine, I was not yet quite sexual.

At school, several cute girlies had their fortune with me in their own dreams. One in particular, or I should say two, was the Beebop twins. They were like marionettes in the corner of our class. Braided redheads, lip gloss, fine teeth, the cross-legged, flirty maneuvers even at that age that would brand them seductresses in adulthood, and their tiny laughs that would turn on a mortician, or at least scare him. They only talked to one another. "Catcha, catcha, catcha," is all I could usually make out of their conversations. They were gorgeous in their undeveloped way. They were carved out of soap. And each of them, almost simultaneously, would divert their vision from the chalkboard to my genitals.

Back in school, Christina Beebop, the smarter of the two twins, sat on the bench during recess while I stood against the wall opposite them. She swiveled her ivory legs and I caught a glimpse of her panties. I was disturbed, drawn, amazed, and my stomach churned like a gastronomic engine. She flipped her thick hair over her shoulder, forever enticing me with those globular eyes and whispering niceties into her sister's ear. Of course, they laughed and stared at me. I had no idea what to do except go up to them one day. I had a wet spot on my crotch, my first sign of a burgeoning manhood. It must've been those damn panties.

"Hello," they said.

"Hi, hi," I said. I stuck my chapped hand into my pocket.

"You dropped mayonnaise on your pants or something," Christina said while chuckling and knowing the stain was something more foreign and terrifying. "I *do* hate those egg sandwiches."

"Me too," I said with my head lowered.

The other one, Jasmine, tried to smell her upper lip. She pushed it toward her nostrils with her index finger. Christina reached over and yanked her sister's finger. "Someone stinks in our class," Jasmine said. She inadvertently started playing with her tiny breasts. "I mean, gosh, they smell like poor people."

"It's probably Joe and Mercy," I said. "They always smell crappy. I don't think they can afford water. They're probably on welfare."

"Ha, ha, ha," they laughed. Their heads rocked in unison like plants blowing in the wind from the stem up.

I thought that I saw three of them. The third twin was a blur or mirage. As I stared in a daze, I felt the same heartburn as when strangers walking by me on the street were covert murderers. It was as if the twins were splitting into three beings, like each of their conjoined lives allowed God to extract the excess memories and mold an entire and final being. On the wall behind the twins was an amateur painting of a distorted and nearly dismembered girl. Her expression was mangled and she nearly frowned. The left arm reached into an impossible dimension. The drawing peered into me. I had just learned the word 'menacing' in Mrs. Male's English class. I blurted out, "Are men actually the Devil if people say they're menacing?"

"Mrs. Male says I'm a beautiful girl," Christina

said, twirling her hair.

"What about me?" Jasmine whimpered.

"Well, you're just like a mirror-image of me, which isn't as beautiful as the real thing."

***

All three of us took to hanging out after school. The first couple of weeks, we mostly sneaked into the movie theater and watch movies all evening. I sat between them. Christina reached for the popcorn tub, which I held for all of us. One time, she dropped kernels onto my crotch. I looked at the kernels. I ate them anyway. Another time, Jasmine reached into the tub and missed. Her hand plopped onto my perfect place. "The kernels are gone," I whispered, munching a bit of burned popcorn. She kept her hand on my lap, and then retracted it with a loud sigh. But even in the dark, I saw she actually smiled. Girls make the obligatory grossed-out sigh when going after boys so they can retain the necessary distance from their male counterparts. Girls can't seem too obvious or slutty. The light from the movie illuminated Jasmine's face and I believed her body didn't really exist. When the movie went dark, I looked over at Christina. Mostly, I smelled her—a baby smell mixed with sweet armpit. I couldn't see her head. I yearned for her bare leg. For sure, it existed somewhere.

I walked them home and stared like a dying dog at Christina—the more beautiful of the twins. "Yeah, you can come in," she said rubbing her nose. "Mama doesn't give a shit." I stumbled into their house, aware of the probable ghosts. Jasmine was behind me with her index finger in my back as if she wielded a pistol. I was never afraid of guns or knives. Christina grabbed my hand and we walked like three train cars into the living room. Their television sat on a footstool and its antennae were wrapped with foil. The electrical cord was plugged into an adaptor that housed many plugs, surely a fire hazard. We plopped onto the tattered couch. We were very, very quiet, but I heard a snoring duet coming from the adjacent bedroom. The home smelled like burned bacon and linoleum cleaner. For the first time in my life, I hovered on a magic carpet over Christina and Jasmine and fussed up their wavy hair with my toes. I was absolutely thrilled. "I think the wild animal show is gonna come on soon," Christina said. She stood up and turned on the television. Jasmine played with my right hand and pulled on each finger as if they would come out of their sockets. I wouldn't have minded if they did.

And then Mama motored into the living room on a three-wheeled vehicle that supported her enormous heft. The vehicle hummed like a boar. She was a pretty woman except for her rolling fat. I forced a smile when I examined Mama's head—it was obtuse, pink in the cheeks, and her face shined. Mama's thick, black hair weighed on her shoulders. "You've brought a friend," Mama said to her girls and grinned. She had all but one of her teeth.

"Oh, Mama!" the twins exclaimed. They ran to her, each girl under one of their Mama's blubbery arms. The girls closed their eyes, opened their nostrils, and took big whiffs of Mama's armpits. She patted the girls' bottoms and swiveled her head as if the sound of their hearts were music. She caressed the girls' backs. "Oh, Mama," they exclaimed again. The girls were delighted felines and just about melted into Mama. They were one beast with four legs sticking out of the side of this enormous, great smelling woman.

Mama turned off the vehicle. She leaned back and looked at me. "What's your name?"

"I'm XX, ma'am.," I said as I suddenly glanced at my holey sneakers.

"No, son, I'm not ma'am. I'm your Mama."

***

One terrible day, I walked home after spending the afternoon in bed with Christina, Jasmine looking in on us. At the end of the afternoon, I left their house again with a splotch of boy-juice on my pants. I whistled in glee as I traipsed home. It was as if I had a girlfriend-and-a-half. Christina's bodily attention, and Jasmine's jealousy, delighted my insides more than ice cream, dad's dirty movies, or pork chops ever could. It was a time of godliness and heavy petting. We tried to keep as quiet as possible so Mama wouldn't notice our moans, but Jasmine was always a secret-crevice away. Her whimpering wasn't disturbing at all, but kind of wonderful: two girls—sisters, no less—desired my body for ungodly reasons. I was their thing and their toy. I loved both of them.

When I unlocked my front door and skipped in, I found my mother and father hacked, dismembered, bloodied, and turned to the simplest of meats.

Their limbs were wrenched into terrifying directions.

Mother was propped up against the wall, a deep gash in her throat.

Father rested what was left of his head on Mother's lap. I sat on the floor not inches away from their dead lives and ruminated for hours, maybe even someone else's lifetime. Flies were birthed and perished during the time I examined my mangled parents. We all have short and terrible lives like flies, I told myself. Were they happy? Were they sad? Did they make it to the gates of Heaven, or were they simply another pair of homeless souls raking through the muck and pond-scum that spanned their murdered, enmeshed minds? I was never sure where they went, except bloodied heavily through our kitchen linoleum. I never knew if their souls shared the worlds and minds of other homeless victims, or if they simply inhabited a swamp invented solely for them by a cruel, godless process of an otherworldly equivalent of evolution.

I was dazed at the knees of their death. I imagined they hugged each other in terror as the hatchet happened upon their heads. They would've gotten a divorce—I know it—but in times of war, husbands and wives put aside their petty hatred and love the beings closest to them. These dead things were my progenitors, the people that propelled me onto this Earth, and now they lay in front of me—their child—as an unfathomable burden. I knew nothing of funerals, death rites, the process of grief and mourning, or where caskets came from.

I didn't even know who my parents' parents were. I was alone in what once was home. And maybe the murderer watched from the stairway. I didn't care. I had known female love by that point. I had experienced what all men yearn for. And then, I actually wished for the hatchet—bring it down on me with the gravity of wild horses, so I too could slog through the death swamp with my only parents, even though they only loved me halfway. *Murderer, oh, murderer,* I repeated in my mind. I wept and tried to be a poet because utterance is demanded in times of mayhem. When there is bloodletting, poets believe they can ease our suffering. Now, in my confined adulthood and barred cell, I'm convinced that poets murder us with their words.

And then I passed out and ended that chapter of my life.

***

I don't remember much else about that time. I do remember now that during the weeks prior to my parents' murder, I had noticed a medium-sized truck idling in front of our house at night. I peeked from behind the drapes, my parents fast asleep, and tried to make out the figures in the vehicle. I seem to remember a fat person and another gaunt figure with a puffy wig. Looking back, I can't help but think those people were involved. The afternoon I found my parents, a fat police officer arrived at my door. I don't know who notified him. He looked at my parents, then at me. He jangled a pair of handcuffs and shook his head. "Looks like foul play," he said.

My house was soon condemned because I was a boy and the foundation of the home was going to pieces. They said they found open pits of damp cement down there as if the foundation had never quite cured.

Needless to say, the whole house and my reality were sinking.

Did I go to a foster home? Did the foster parents molest me? Or did the police simply store me in a closet made for pirates and terrorists?

The police eventually turned me over to a Russian woman, if I remember correctly. She wore a furry, dead animal around her neck and a puffy hat. The woman smiled, took my hand and I went into the cab of her truck. I remember looking at the façade of some institutional building as we drove away.

The Russian woman reassured me in her accented English—always smiling, putting her gaunt hand on my lap and emanating a department store fragrance—that I would be loved.

I don't recall going to my parent's funeral, but I have a vague image of viewing the blue-green body of my mother in her casket. Brows plucked, dress not fondled, a rose in her hand, closed lids, a body like dry ice. I may have kissed her. She was dense like a sack stuffed with Kryptonite. I was a small, small boy.

I don't know if it was the stress of the murders, or some effect on my immune system, but my spine was filled with some gorgeous bacteria. I grew out-of-sync with time. I'd be sitting with my legs twining like forks in an office of child welfare, then I'd be asleep in a stranger's bed. And then, I'd be hot and full of phlegm—a fever like a mosquito net in the blazing desert. Finally, I'd find myself walking against the flow of crowds in the business districts of invented cities. I grew in and out of my clothes. My hair was simultaneously short and long. Doctors said I had flighty blood sugar, inept glandular waste, spores in many vital organs, and a tendency toward dissociative fugues. I'd wake up in municipalities having procured aliases for myself, both male and female.

***

One day, Mama came to pick me up from a shanty town just over the state border. I was in an orphanage or meat locker for zombies. Grindings and fingernail scratches blanketed the walls of the shack, as if the children had tried to eat their way out. The authorities were nice enough to me. I was fed bologna sandwiches and milk. I blurted out Latin or imagined languages. I fell into inexplicable slumbers and the authorities somehow knew I had a sick spine and severe problems with memory. I wore a grandfather suit, enormous dress shoes, a carnation in my lapel, white socks, cologne, and had braces. But I always had perfect teeth! I never had a cavity, nor do I remember seeing an oral surgeon. Perhaps it was a psychiatrist who thought that tightening me tooth-and-mouth would prevent my mind from fracturing further.

The authorities eventually handed me over to Mama. Mama waited for me on her three-wheeled vehicle in the dimly-lit hallway of the orphanage. I wept seeing her and hugged her enormous fat. I buried my head in her breasts and she caressed my head and soothed me. She wore a preposterous silk maneuver over her body. It was like cowhide with floral designs and sweet odor. I loved the cowhide. I loved Mama.

"Let's go home," Mama said.

I climbed into an ancient and dusty limousine that was chauffeured by a tall gentleman with a deformed head. Somehow, Mama managed to cram into an undisclosed door of the limo. I couldn't see but her monstrous silhouette through a soiled screen, but I could hear her voice well. What she said is beyond me. Utterance wavering out of my existence for minutes, sometimes hours, at a time. Her voice was a foghorn in the distance and inside the limo at the same time. And I noticed at some point that Christine and Jasmine didn't come with Mama. And even if they had come with, I was afraid they were now middle-aged.

The gentleman with the deformed head who drove the car turned out to be Papa. He was pleasant enough and carried me into their home. I was weak-kneed and my body was a melting ice sculpture. They did set me up with my own bed in a room I didn't know even existed. Papa nourished me and spooned various soups into my mouth through a span of time.

He brushed my teeth and mornings blended together into a series of faces hovering over me... the hypnotizing sound of my breath as Papa took my temperature again and again. Papa put his working-man hands on my shins. I grew thinner and harder to pin down. He told me all I needed was sleep. Papa assured me he had procured a medical degree of some sort and was an expert on bile and miasma. Papa put pillows under my feet, showered me, shampooed my hair and whatever else. I must've trusted the man. I had no other choice.

And then Christina entered my bedroom. At first, she stuck her head in to get a glimpse of the boy-ghost. God, at least she was still my age. I tried to muster a smile and hope she remembered caressing me. *Please do that again,* I pleaded with her in my mind. She crept in and I did realize that her shoulders and face had changed ever-so-slightly. Indeed, she started to turn womanly, but she comforted me nonetheless. Perhaps I, too, had begun to evolve into a man. But this, I truly doubted. I truly believed I was trapped in childhood.

I asked Christina if Jasmine still lived at home, and she laughed. At first, I was angered because I thought she was laughing about my very soul, but she said Jasmine had visited me the previous day. Didn't I remember? Jasmine had played cards with me. *Oh, of course,* I lied. I faded in and out of the soup of dusk, but she remained by my side with a book. Occasionally, she flew above me and kissed my forehead.

I caught a glimpse of her breasts. They, too, had transformed. They had more potential as lures and bait. Men would soon pray to her breasts, but I believed they were mine.

I asked Christina if there were other people living in the house. She closed the book and shook her head. She wanted to know why I had asked. "Well," I told her. "Sometimes, weighted shadows pass by my bedroom. Although the shadows are clothed in something like burlap, I can never make out any of their faces. But I know they're looking at me—spying on me, even."

Christina covered her petite mouth with her hand. I couldn't quite tell if she was giggling. "You just get some beauty sleep, OK?"

***

Papa talked to one of the burlap shadows outside of my bedroom one day. What they mumbled to each other was top secret—my health and the health of the county depended on it.

I was just out of my zillionth slumber. It definitely lasted an hour or a day. My head was a cement bag and my neck would break soon. Floral sheets covered all of my windows. And the porridge Papa fed me began to taste like malaria.

Mama had given me a fly swatter to keep my reflexes occupied. I wielded it like a weapon at all times—entranced by flies doing figure eights around my breath. Sometimes, I splattered one or two. This gave me a sense of pride and purpose. The bible says we all need the purpose of godliness during our short lives. At least I had maggots and flies to maim.

The heavy and thick-bearded shadows walked back-and-forth past my bedroom. I'm sure they were simply friends of the family. Or enemies they had no choice but to let in. Whatever the case, the light was poor in our home. I had been sick for centuries, at least. I believed I lived with Dracula and was his bastard son. I was deprived of blood and grew sick—hence the porridge Papa fed me with the flavor of malaria. I began to vent my anger by swatting at the man-shadows as big as fear right outside my bedroom door. Of course, I couldn't elongate my arm enough to splatter their 2-D heads. I simply pretended they were close, the way the moon is a tram's ride away. I, too, could splatter their 2-D heads against the walls and finally uncover what's inside shadows.

I didn't know what Papa was saying about me to one of the larger shadows. The shadow was taller and more masculine than Papa and had a deep voice. They mumbled back and forth as if they were feeding each other thread.

I was convinced they were speaking about me.

At times, the sunlight burned the darkness away from Papa's face as he hovered over me, feeding me thickened malaria. And he was an ugly man with a head like a forceps baby; brittle hair; skin worse than paraffin; but perfectly straight teeth. His teeth were square, white, acutely proportioned. He was a medical professional, so this made sense. He always wore a lab coat, as if my bedroom was an extension of his laboratory.

The masculine shadow was just outside of

light's reach. I made out Papa nodding and I thought I understood phrases like, "And how are the boy's molars and canines?" and "You absolutely sure he's THE ONE?" and Papa replied, "My twins have the gift of bloodhounds for sniffing out the boys with promising genes."

I closed my eyes. They waded in and out of my mind. All things and all people were broth. I opened my eyes as Papa passed a large, glass jar to the burlap, masculine shadow who, I was convinced, had a malicious disposition.

I shook my weighty head and I hoped they couldn't hear my brains jiggling. I remember clearly, now, there were terrifying meats inside that jar!

Over the years since, I've pictured bulbous meats and blushing skins inside the jar as a cube of a wild boar. That's simply how my mind has revealed the jar's innards to me. It surely was cubed and gangrenous fleshes inside that jar. The afternoon I first saw the jarred meats, Papa and a small crowd of shadows exchanged phrases and disturbances, but I only caught, "I hope the meat wasn't named yet."

***

One morning, I happened out of an ill, ill slumber that forced me to stand. I could barely bear my weight at that period in my life. I was determined and grinded my perfect teeth—now without braces—and gathered the wherewithal to slop one foot in front of the other until I arrived in the living room. Papa was nearly buried in his recliner and glared right through me as I entered their room. Christina and Jasmine were huddled up against their Mama. She was, subsequently, pinned to the couch.

The couch was about to sink through the floor.

Everyone stopped whispering once they saw me. I wiped my eyes and tried to put on a pleasant grin even though I sensed things were terribly wrong. The sun threw shadows against the dirty walls. There was an odor of pipe smoke. My pants were not buttoned properly and my shirt was hanging out. Some diseased porridge had landed on my chest—for how long, I could never determine. My gums were in searing pain and I tasted cod in my elderly mouth. I forgot the names of the seasons or how old I was.

"We just had breakfast," Papa exclaimed, composing himself. "Didn't we, family?"

"There were some people looking for you," Christina blurted out before her head went back to into Mama's bosom.

"Shush, girl," Mama said.

"We just warmed up some milk," Papa said a bit too excitedly. Cheap smoke billowed from his bassoon-shaped pipe.

"I thought I smelled... cinnamon... or some rodeo," I added.

Each and every one of them chuckled as if to criticize my very soul.

"It was a cop and maybe his Russian wife looking for you," Christina added. Mama swatted her dense little head, even though she would never truly harm her daughter.

"You hungry?" Mama asked me. She gently pushed Christina's face away. "You must be malnourished after all this time."

"The boy should be fine," Papa reiterated with a reprimanding look on his face. "We did give him the porridge, Ma." Smoke escaped and doubled against the ceiling.

Again, each of them chuckled even though Papa gave them a look of the coroner.

I tried to smile. "Tastes like I've been chewing bugs."

"Don't say that, son" Mama exclaimed trying to stand up. The unfathomable gravity of her mass had long since repressed her. "There's still nourishment in the pot, right, Christina?"

"The kitchen is that way, if you can't remember" Jasmine said and pointed. "You have a blank look like you've been away from this world." She drooled, but quickly sopped it up with her shirtsleeve.

"The fat cop and his Russian wife sat there for quite some time," Christina said as she faced me. "At the kitchen table... right over there..."

"Christina," Papa said as he placed the smoldering pipe on the coffee table. He had a stern jaw as if his head might pop off in a second or two. "Just shut..." and he calmed down by strumming a finger through his thin hair and pomade. "You don't need to know and he don't have to do with this," he muttered as if I couldn't hear or understand.

I wanted to re-button my pants, but it would look vile and impolite. Etiquette, even during a crisis, is demanded by the Lord who betrays us, even. "I'll be alright," I swallowed hard. "Papa's right. There was the delicious porridge." I turned toward the wire-framed man who would cock a pistol in a second if he believed you were posing to be smarter than him. "I didn't mean anything about the bugs."

Papa lightened up then, and chuckled. He picked up his pipe and puffed and puffed. At about that time, a voice came over his radio. The voice enunciated numbers and code like, "72... 69... 86... 104."

"Don't be silly," Papa said. "You do need some nourishment. I know that porridge wasn't enough. Plus, you were chucking it back up half the time, anyway." His sweet pipe smoke made me ill. "Don't you want some warm milk?"

Christina lifted her fattened face from Mama's tits. There was wetness on Mama's pullover and some kind of human pooling. Unnatural. "The cop explained he's been looking for a boy about your size and shape," Christina said.

"Tina!" Papa nearly yelped at that precise moment. He lowered his voice—again convinced I was too ruined to hear detail and rage. "The backhand? Remember the backhand?"

"That's not gonna happen at this day and age," Christina responded. "Right, Mama?"

Mama petted her favorite daughter's head again and again. Christina looked feline, goddess-like. If I could have children with her—or if they would simply let me hover and fly over once every month—I could be sustained.

Papa's face balled-up and was tightening in on itself.

"They simply had some questions for you since... your mommy and daddy went... unfortunate... isn't that right, Mama?" I could tell Mama was blushing, embarrassed, and even a bit enraged—but this, here, was the offspring of some divine being, at least in Mama's obese eyes. Christina could do no wrong, even in the presence of Papa and the Lord.

The voice on the radio came in sharp once again: "113... 45... 986... 1765..." And then it faded. What kind of code was it? I imagined they were coordinates—like where Saturn, Venus and the moon would stand in concert with the sinister plans of some hit man... or they were delivering classified genetic code... some genes of a yet-to-be discovered species— part elephant, dinosaur, homo sapien and succubus...

Any of those choices—whichever and when— almost let the urine out. To this day, I can't tell you why. But I imagine, now, it went something like this: legislators and psychics alike have proclaimed that witnessing the slaughter of one's ancestry will put the hex and evil eye directly onto the muscle of the heart; and even force the ghost out of the observer's body and into a gas can somewhere, or a fire extinguisher, or, worse, into some other being alto- gether. I am that boy with his soul locked inside a canteen from the Civil

War, or a tomb in a forgotten desert, or in some endangered species of boar that protects the last of its kind, terrified that it thinks human thoughts. And it was my genetic code the voice cascaded into the county's ether—not out of empathy, but out of unexplained harm...

Again, Papa put his pipe on the table next to his recliner and scratched the stubble on his chin. That sandpaper sound was louder than the whole room. "Why don't you squeeze in there next to the girls, son? Mama won't mind. Go on," he said to me, commanding me with his crooked finger. "Go on." He laughed and suckled on his pipe some more.

Yes, I squeezed in, I believe. I do recall and recount. There was Christina and Jasmine both up into the bosom of their Mama, and was commanded to meld with girl pups and become one with Mama and all that comes out...

***

I woke up at some point afterward, having splayed all my limbs onto the couch's inches. Mama and the girls were long gone. It was a dark room and time. Papa reclined in his chair, pipe in his mouth, speaking code into the radio receiver. As I refocused my eyes, I discovered he was staring right at me as he communicated with a woman with a foreign accent.

She sounded eerily familiar, but from which lifetime, I have yet to discern.

Papa watched over me as if I may evaporate. He informed, "The implant hasn't been successful." He rocked and spewed out smoke and evil. "Christina assures me he *is* THE ONE. I have no choice but to trust... She has THE GIFT."

That female foreign voice screeched out indecipherable rage—the rage of an age-old anthropologist who's discovered the wild beast which would ensure riches and eternity.

"His lineage has been followed for more than a decade... I assure you *all* was taken care of readily." I had never seen him shake that way. Even the pipe smoke was afraid.

My hand protected my boyhood groin.

My area was sore. Yes, I was embarrassed because I couldn't help but soothe with my right hand. It wasn't the pleasure of release. I simply needed to acknowledge my soreness with human touch, even though it was simply mine. Aching from what, I didn't want to imagine. It wasn't the kind of groin I wanted anymore. It was reddened groin, much like that of a retired merchant at sea who has betrothed a prostitute too many. A man regrets his groin under those circumstances, but at least that man is old and can reflect upon his tyranny over women as he awaits his own death.

I had nothing to consciously treasure about any girl, even the one I believed I loved. I know I hovered over her, and she over me, and there was even some avid groping. But our nudity didn't even approach these kinds of consequences. I had the groin of a corpse who aches as he decomposes.

"I assure you," Papa said in between puffs, "the implant will take this time."

The woman's howl went from foreign to our nation's most feared form of discourse: "It fucking better." And then, static.

Papa leaned defeated into his faux leather recliner. The pipe was empty, but I couldn't tell if his face was. Yes, he was a wire-thin man who could box his way out of Hell, but that demon on the other hand had a clutch on his heart. And it was female.

***

"Is this the boy?" the cop asked, pointing at me.

He wore a khaki uniform and medals across his lapel. We were forever in the living room. I was exhausted and it had been a lifetime since I witnessed the meats of parents. It's funny now, but I had hoped to envision their meats again, as if confronting them could cure me of my present circumstance.

I had dried milk all over my rotten face.

It was winter. I wore yellowed thermal underwear, two coats, no socks and a hillbilly's grin. I was sprawled on the couch like a drunken serf.

"You lost your Mama and Papa a while back?" the cop asked me while darting his eyes between Mama and me. She sat on her three-wheeled vehicle, as fat as ever.

"Yeah, that's him, James," she said.

"He doesn't look like he could massacre nobody." The cop fiddled with one of his medals and put his hands on his hips.

The handcuffs jangled.

The cop, too, was fucking fat. "Hell, you're a good kid from what they tell me."

"Yes, sir," I said. The dried milk was chapping my face. Milk on the face is a joy for infants, but a horror for a boy my age. I didn't want a fucking chapped face or any family anymore. I wanted back my ghost from the canteen or tomb or the wild boar. What the hell is a pig going to do with human thoughts? I was so goddamned empty.

So I wiped my mouth with my sleeve.

"Did the boy stick his hand inside the jar?" the cop asked.

"Didn't observe," Papa retorted. His hands were tightly in his pockets.

The radio started its numerology again.

I looked at my feet and hoped they were transmitting my genetic code into the county's ether.

Christina sat next to me and began caressing my scalp. I loved that and always will. She dug her fingernails into my head and kissed me fully and she had a thin fragrance.

And I suddenly flashed to the image of Christina screaming while on the marble slab. Her legs were split wide open as if she were giving birth. Papa and the crowd of shadows did put a gown on her. Obese Mama was actually standing—but barely—and held her favorite daughter's hand. I knew it wasn't the first time, and probably wouldn't be the last. One of the weighty, masculine shadows shrieked, "*Another fucking girl!*"

I returned to the present as Christina caressed my face and I knew, then, I didn't have anything left in me to give her.

I couldn't give her THE BOY.

The cop continued to jangle his handcuffs. "You're a good boy, right?" he asked, showing his perfectly square teeth to me. They were almost transparent. A row of transparent teeth, hard as Kryptonite, planted in the gums of a cop! His teeth were the work of a master. The cop nodded. "You're good?"

Mama turned off her vehicle. "James, you got nothing to worry about here."

"Yes, sir," I said.

"He's got no business peeking into the formaldehyde, Mama." The cop sucked in air through his Kryptonite teeth.

Christina lay her head on my shoulder and I could hear her begin to weep.

"The way his mommy and daddy was slaughtered and hacked and chucked—you know, *that* thing!" The cop practically stripped one of the medals from his lapel as he exhorted. "Nobody... I mean *nobody*... can know it was me."

"Reassure Greta that the implant *will* take, James," Papa pleaded. "I'm sure of it. I'd put my life on the line." He swallowed hard as if he regretted that admission. "Christina says it's so." He cradled the glass canister with the chucked meats in it. The spiraled, chunked, and bitten meats in the jar shook among the horrible juice. "Here you go, James," Papa said.

"Thank you." The cop said as he confiscated the jar.

Christina had her palm on my groin, and hadn't noticed until then. I regretted I didn't notice. It was sore and she took her palm away. She might as well have lopped off her lovely hand and launched it into outer space.

Christina strolled over to her Mama with arms extended and weeping. She just about sprinted to Mama. They hugged. I turned away from love and comfort and toward the ancient black-and-white TV. It was obese, the way Mama was obese. Jasmine huddled behind the TV with her knees up to her chest and her hair over her face. She wept, too. All the females wept. I attempted to give her a look of great empathy, even though it was my groin on the butcher's block.

"I want a baby, too!" Jasmine exclaimed.

***

Of course, the cop took me away that night. At first, they took me to the local precinct. It wasn't bad at all. I turned on the TV as I lay on a cot. A Russian woman who wore her hair in pigtails walked into the room. She wore rouge and I thought she was preparing for her own funeral. I had no idea who she was. She sat at my feet and grinned.

She had yellow teeth.

"Can I have some coffee?" I asked.

She stared at me blankly for what must've been ten minutes. She had no pupils and didn't blink. "You touched through the formaldehyde?"

"I would never touch anyone through formal-dehyde, ma'am." I knew what she was referring to, but

64

why the hell would I want to touch chucked and spiraled meats soaked in formaldehyde? I mean, the meats belonged to Christina and me. But I, in no way, wanted to own those meats. I was terrified. "Who told you this?"

"It's in the evidence," she said in a monotone, thickly accented voice.

"It's not my fault. I didn't touch any meats. I swear to God, ma'am. You can give me a lie detector test. I'm telling you, you can have the meats."

"We already gave you the detector." She tilted her head to her side. "Why are you guilty? Don't you want to give us a BOY?"

"It's not my fault! It was them crazy fuckers! I wanted to make a son for you," I said.

The woman just looked at me.

Two uniformed officers entered the room. The fat one with the medals pinned to his lapel turned off the TV. "Are you done with him?" they asked in unison.

The woman never took her eye off me, but her face was lifeless and caked onto her skull.

"He is guilty of checking the formaldehyde meats for the gender. He must provide for us THE BOY."

They handcuffed me and whisked me away for the last time.

*****

I was stripped of all my clothes and belongings; blindfolded and put into one van; exited; put into another van; and was driven in figure-eights and zigzags. When they finally arrived at my new living quarters and yanked me out of the van, I caught a glimpse of a wooden sign at the entrance from under my blindfold: *GOLDMINE, 1893* it said.

I was escorted into an old-fashioned elevator. The officer slammed the gate shut and we started to descend and descend. The elevator hummed and shuttered the whole way down. Occasionally, we passed a dim, yellow light attached to the wall of the shaft. It took more than twenty-seven minutes to reach the bottom.

It's now thirteen years later and I lie on my pristine and well-kempt cot. The sparkling, white walls drone, or maybe that's actually inside me. There is nothing to look at in my world. The overhead lights are on twenty-four hours a day. The twin guards have treated me very well. I'm not sure when they leave or when they arrive. They may actually live outside of my door. And I've grown to like the lukewarm porridge they feed me.

I'm sure I will never see sunlight or wear clothes ever again.

There's a speaker that hangs from the back corner of my cell. Every day at the same time (although, what time or day or month it is, I haven't a clue) a real woman's voice emanates from the speaker and recites a script to keep me in the mood at all times: "Hey, there, pretty boy! You know I've been thinking about you *all night*. Now, lotion up those manly hands of yours and handle that lovely groin... not too much, though... We wouldn't want you to drain *any* of those children... and while doing that, think of *me*, the *only* person in the world who loves you... and *your* woman *needs* a BOY... She *needs* one bad..." Sometimes, she'll go on. Don't get me wrong, I yearn to hear her throaty, whore's voice. But she hardly wavers from the script. It has long ago lost most of its effect. I tried to tell them that once—that every man needs variety, actual sentiment, a *reaction*.

But I don't think they can hear my voice.

And what I believe is every twenty-one days or so, the twin guards escort an absolutely stunning woman into my cell. She's the only person I have left. I mean, I can't begin to tell you about her fragrance and the lightness of her hair; her deeply set eyes; the exoticism; the wildness of her expressions.

She has no name.

And she may not be entirely human.

This goddess always undresses seductively as if this were the first time we met, or even the first time I've seen a woman's pubis. Her smile is big; the lips are as red as the meats I've witnessed throughout my life; and even her tears that trickle down her cheeks each time are endearing.

She hardly ever says anything spontaneous or responds to any of my questions. She says the things they believe I want to hear in order to be properly aroused.

"I'm *so* sorry for all this," she said one time. I'll never forget it. I barely heard her. I'm not sure she wanted me to hear, but I grasped that she needed to express this. She *needed* to tell me.

She climbs on top of me. The rule is this: I must remain absolutely still and envision—with all of my masculine ambition—a strong, strong baby BOY. Her mouth heads directly to arousing my various parts. The faces of Christina and Jasmine meld with this woman's face each time we engage in the act. Mostly, I *am* able to redirect my attention toward the potentiality of THE BOY.

If THE BOY ever does arrive, I'm not sure where he'll live or what he'll do. I gather he's needed with the entire weight of someone's government.

Even if he will be my son, I don't care one bit.

Because right here and now, this nameless woman's fragrance is absolutely unbearable!

And I've *finally* begun to love her.

END TRAM

Several hours before sunrise: I was recording ants. I had set up a soft but adequate light and had placed my video camera on a tripod. I tried not to purge too violently the network of leaves and worms and beetles. I prodded the ground with my walking stick. (Everything looks yellowed through a lens.) There was a kind of hyphenated, miniature creek (in the shape of a cross) that an arrow-shot of ants was crawling over. They had built a twig bridge. And over that bridge, they crossed and they gripped in their mouths blurbs of nourishment: leafy triangles, bit chunks, even crickets. I had been studying the phero-mone trails (scents they give off), through which these particular ants seemed to be leaving sort of communicative remnants (or, a chemical syntax that would be equivalent to a human colony's complicated trail of crumpled paper-balls on which are bits of speech, survival anecdotes, etc.). Humidity hung like a ghoul among the vines. I had gotten more than an hour of footage of this fleeting parade, had gathered some specimens, when I heard the first rumble below the ground. I put my fist on a tree next to me (gripping the tripod with the other hand), and thought perhaps it was an earthquake. I stopped the videotape. I sat (not worried about bugs walking up my pant leg for just one moment), and heard it again. It was dull and under-ground. Deep, deep. There were no moans, no panic of hands that I pictured in my mind, no cries for help. I reached for my thermos. Sipped warm coffee with my pointy tongue. I was there. Maybe twenty minutes passed. (I had just begun to record ants again.) And the two men walked toward me out of the mid-part of the swamp.

The man in front was unhideous. He held the other man's hand, and the other man was dragging a wooden box by a rope that was tied to his waist. The man in front (who wore a flannel shirt and muddy boots) stopped and gaped as he saw me with my camera. *I am only taping ants and sampling phero-mones*, I thought in my head. Then he lurched back, stopping the other man (who wore a black suit jacket, black pants, a square haircut as if he were wearing a box on his head, and had a beard without a mustache), and smiled in relief. "I'm Ember," he said to me. "I think we're lost." The other man was sipping his teeth, paring the slowly reddening sky with his eye slits.

I parted from my camera (making a mental note that it was pointing directly at this couple), and wiped my grimy hands on my jeans. "Hi," I said. "You've just come out of the mid-part of the swamp." I reached out to shake hands with Ember.

Ember unclasped his grip from the other man. He signed to him. The other man signed back. "Yes," Ember said. "We have figured this out." I know a bit of sign language, but I didn't recognize what they were gesturing to one another. They made rectangular shapes in the air with their fingers, sometimes cupping their hands close to their bodies, nodding, making more rectangles and domes, crooking their necks, shaking. Ember turned back to me. "This is Clip. He is deaf-mute, I believe."

Clip looked at me with those eye slits. My soft but adequate light highlighted this man's rickety shape. He was bony, cloaked by his formal garb, and smelled. He nodded to me and formed more rectangles in the air and finished his sentence by hugging his two fists close to his liver.

I waved.

Ember smiled, almost embarrassingly, and muttered. "He asked you why you are videotaping." He again tugged at Clip's hand as if he were trying to keep the man from fleeing. Clip grasped the rope that was connected to his wooden box.

I became self-conscious of my camera. To me, it was small and not intrusive. It looked like a steel butterfly. "I'm just taping bugs. I'm an entomologist."

I tried not to stare, but locked my eyes on Clip's box. It was beaten and warped. There seemed to be nails jammed through each of its edges to keep it forever closed. I could not tell (because it was still somewhat dark out) what kind of wood it was composed of. I imagined (in a moment of quiet and nervousness that, for me, makes me go wandering veiny through my thinking) that he had recovered the sealed box from a cloudy pool of muck; that the box had, perhaps, been lying there for a decade or two trying to resist decomposition in order for some person to find it. The rope was connected to the box by a thick, rusty ring. The rope, too, was thick and falling apart. It reached up in spindly twines toward Clip's waist.

I was kicking rocks. I had forgotten about the ants. Then, I remembered the quake I had felt earlier. "Did you guys feel that shaking a bit ago?" I asked nervously.

Clip started to draw rectangles and domes. He moved his hands swiftly, maniacally. But Ember tugged hard at his arm. Clip stopped.

"We didn't feel anything," Ember said. He made one signal in the air to his companion without looking at him. "We sure did not."

I sat on a medium-sized rock. "It was strange because I heard a rumbling from the direction you guys were headed." I turned around and pointed.

I looked back at Clip. He stared at me, arms at his side, like a stake in the ground. It was unnerving. I could see his chest move in and out as he breathed. He kept making attempts to raise his hands (to communicate), but dropped them as if he thought it was better not to. Ember was gripping Clip's arm, squeezing, really. The light shone on them. Things were creaking in the background, small masses groping about the damp swamp floor, some thousands of species. I glanced at the box again. I had thought to ask them where they were headed, how they got lost. But I gritted my teeth. I stuck my hands in my pockets. (I knew there was a small carving blade in there.) My shoe was untied, but I thought it could be dangerous to bend down and tie it. The sun was very slow to come, it seemed to me. Every thought I had was inadequate. I did not care where they were from, where they were going. I wanted Ember to let go. I wanted Clip's tongue to correct itself and blurt.

"We're trying to... meet up with some people... that we got separated from." Ember began to fiddle with something around his belt loop. An object. I could not tell. I could not tell. There was a clicking sound. (Metal?) It was definitely a cocking, clicking sound. He breached the humid silence with his uncanny, full-of-square-teeth grin. It was big. "You know," Ember said, suddenly opening up. "Weird to have a fascination with bugs. Don't you think?" He looked up into my camera. "I once had a nine year old girlfriend when I was eight who loved the feel of a good caterpillar frolicking across her palm. Not that *you* look anything like her. She was a finicky, pink little girl. She used to tickle my throat-part with her quipping tongue. Oh, it was love. 'Platoon of legs,' she'd say about the caterpillars. A whole nest of them (maybe a thousand) blossomed along our road and crawled up our house walls one summer. (The summer she was tickling my throat a whole bunch.) 'Platoon of legs.' Was her dad in the military? I do not know. But *he* was a gun hog. He could hog a pistol (whether it be revolver, scoped rifle, elephant killer, shotgun, automatic, musket), he could hog a pistol. Shit. He could riff with a pistol up against any qualm (human, boar, or even his beloved horse) and pull on the damn thing with a gallant smile. Ha!" I noticed then that he was signing to Clip with his right hand down around his thigh as if he did not want me to see. His fingers were drafting whole paintings. I did not know if he was signing to Clip, or if he was translating for him. "A rather loon. But his daughter, the finicky, pink spiff of love I had when I was eight, was a gem, a bug lover, from a, what should I say, wretched family? I think they were all, at their core, bug lovers."

My legs were twining. I was nervous. I could not think of a sentence or an adequate question. I felt like I must think of something. I could not ask if they were from this state. I could not ask if they were brothers. I could not ask if Clip was really a deaf-mute. I could not ask if their sign language was the genuine thing, or some artifice. "I am simply entranced... by ants." My legs stopped twining.

"Ah," Ember said. "To study microbes would have been my call. But my college was too quaint."

I lightened for a moment. "What did you study?"

"I dropped out of examining Julius Caesar."

"Julius..."

There was another rumble.

"See! Did you hear that?"

Clip began to do small jumps in place. His hands went up making those (now almost wrenching) hieroglyphs.

Ember pulled out his gun. He opened it. "I have only one bullet left. That is a quandary. When there are seven billion people in the world and you have only one bullet left, that is a bad morning. The sun spoils my fun continually. Oh, quandaries. Mr. Bug Lover, have you ever heard of the Amtrak Migrations? It is a rather terrible movement of a whole slew of people like Clip from the swamps to Canada. We are on our way to Canada. What you heard was a... train. What you see here in Clip is a Swamp Tramp. They all dress in this formal garb of black. They all have large Adam's apples, even the women. I am one among many who are *guiding* these folk to Canada. I cannot tell you what is in Canada. I cannot tell you why we are taking them there. I cannot tell you where the Swamp Tramps are from. I cannot tell you how many there are." Ember lifted his gun first toward me, then pointed it toward the darkness, quivering. "Clip has a very unique form of sign." Ember lit a cigarette and drew with his hands as if to signal for Clip to begin his show.

Clip began to sign frantically at me. I knew Clip could not express himself to me. As he realized his signing was futile, he mouthed particular airs and gestured with his right hand as if he were pinching salt. There was silence. He glanced at Ember (as if he wanted Ember to translate his thoughts), bobbing his head, thinking and mouthing whole vacuous sentences. (These sentences are now quite lost.) Then, after his white, white peeling face blushed out of frustration, he slowly constructed buildings in the air with his hands—his syntax, his architecture.

"This is not sign language," Ember said, fiddling with his pistol. "Do you know what the name of their language is?" He made that full-of-square-teeth grin. I knew things were becoming hopeless. "In English, we call their language 'The Bolshoi Moskow Circus,' or simply 'The Moscow.' What he is drawing in the air are the shapes of the terrific stone churches, golden domes, cathedrals, and chapels of Moscow. Each structure he draws (depending upon where in the air he draws it in relation to his liver), represents a different meaning."

Clip was magnificent with his chapped hands. Each hand looked like an adobe hut with five digits for chimneys. His face remained fugue-like and pale. What was he trying to tell me? Was he warning me? Was there a bunch of Swamp Tramps in a train-crash out in the mid-part of the swamp? Were they all miming 'The Moscow' to would-be rescuers, to the peopleless dawn, to their captors?

"The organizing principle for their grammar is spatial," Ember continued. "Shit." He dragged on his sixth cigarette. His gun lay on his lap. "Their grammar is organized by the spatial layout of the arena of the Bolshoi Moskow Circus. Can you imagine the arena? It is a hat-like dome with a zigzag brim that goes around the structure. But that is only the part that was visible above ground. Underground (which is the organizing principle for their language) were five substitute arenas: equestrian, illusionist, ice, water, and luminous. Say he were to draw the Church of Anna's Conception in the illusionist arena (which is three centimeters away from his heart), then drag his index finger through the air diagonally to the water arena (which is four centimeters away from his liver), this would signal, *We are in danger*."

Clip was drawing a building. (I have watched this 749 times on my videotape since last summer. He drew a dome-like thing with a swift brush of his pinky, then drew what I took to be several triangular windows—all near his heart. He then dragged his index finger through the air like a pointer and constructed the same figure near his liver. He kept stomping his booted foot against the ground.)

"And they don't even know that Moscow used to exist. Ain't that a goddamned thing?"

"Are you going to shoot me?" I asked.

"There were 677 churches that used to exist in Moscow. There are five spatial categories to their language. That's 3,385 characters. If they draw one building in one area, then drag their hands to another area and draw the building again, that's a sentence. And so on."

"Are you going to shoot me?"

Ember cocked his gun. "Why would I shoot you? You're in love with bugs."

We are in danger.

We are in danger.

The man in front (Ember) held the other man's hand (Clip) and tied to that man's waist was a wooden box that he dragged (we are in danger). The box was jammed with nails to its edges like it was supposed to be sealed forever. It looked warped and ravaged, like it had been sucked out of the swamp. Maybe it wasn't. They idled past me. The man in front looked at my video camera as the other man made signs with his hands. This man was dressed in a black suit jacket, black pants, and had a beard without a mustache. It was morning now. I waited for about ten minutes then followed their footsteps through the muck. They left good prints. I carried my camera. I had plenty of tape left. I followed them. I do not know how long I trekked. But I finally got to an opening, a clearing. I stood there and had forgotten this is where the Mississippi used to be. How dry, infirm, a cracked wooden riverbed, not like land we usually know, nor like some kind of moon, but just more than arid. It was deep and perhaps deeper. This is where the Mississippi used to be, and now there was this endless route of train cars linked by rings and articulations. This train sat in tracks embedded in the riverbed. The Mississippi spanned 2,350 miles. I could not count the cars. I could not see an engine. There was somewhere between one car and a number greater than the biggest number that I could imagine. It would ferret north and perhaps further than that. There were oodles of black-jacketed men encrypting buildings with their chapped hands in the air. These men also had beards and no mustaches. There were women doing the same thing. There were children. I did not hear gunshots, cries, shoving, slaps, or thuds. There was a coal-burning smell. There was smoke spiraling upward from what I counted as 46 steel, vertical gullies, making the shapes of Egypt, Persia, Macedonia, etc., in the sky. I set up my camera again and began to tape. (Everything looks yellowed through a lens.) I am not a superstitious man. I am an entomologist. The man in front (Ember), had called me a bug lover. He, too, was in love with a bug lover when he was eight years old. She was a pink, finicky girl who tickled his throat with her tongue. This man in front dragged another man (Clip) who dragged a wooden box. This man made buildings with his hands that were his way-of-saying. This man was somewhere. In front of me was an expanse of train. Clip was in every train-car. Clip made transient maps. (The smoke churned and funneled up in the air, and the thing began to move, move.) Clip spanned 2,350 miles. I set up my camera. Several hours after sunrise: I was recording ants.

FOOD

Oscar puts one of her faded sun dresses into a box marked *Things* and fishes through all her other clothes. He can still smell her. Faint like shampoo. He touches his forehead. "Damn," he mumbles. It's been a year since his wife, Norma, died. Alongside the television are seven boxes filled with clothes, old combs, rosaries, and knickknacks. It's seven in the morning.

Michael is another story. He tried to talk to his son when it first happened. "Look, I know you miss your mom." Michael's face has turned red as if he's been holding his breath all this time. He's not much more than skin and bones and looks as if he might blow over. "If you won't talk to me, I can't help you." He used to be the most boisterous kid in school. Aggressive, even. Now, he draws and sits in his room most of the time. "You think too much, Michael."

One time, about six months ago, he went into Michael's room and found one of his wife's bras tangled in with the bed covers. When Michael got home from school, Oscar shoved the bra in his face. "What the hell is this? You know what this is?"

Michael didn't say anything.

"Damn, you don't talk to me no more... don't eat. What the hell's wrong with you?"

"You think I'm a homo, huh?"

Oscar was taken aback and ran his fingers through his hair. "No... I mean, I don't know. You gotta tell me what's going on with you."

"I'm not a homo."

Something about this infuriated him. He dropped his cigarette. "She was my wife, goddamn it! You ever think of that?"

***

A few weeks ago, Michael came into his room at 2 a.m., wrapped in a fuzzy, blue blanket. Oscar was lying in bed having just snubbed his fourth cigarette of the night. He couldn't sleep.

"Dad, can I stay in here tonight?"

Oscar wiped his eyes and took a good look at his son. He was twelve and probably didn't weigh more than ninety pounds. "Can't sleep?"

"There's somebody at my window. Or at the back door."

"Really?" Oscar sat up and reached in between the mattress.

"I hear him scratching. He has real long nails. He goes through our garbage cans."

"You seen him?"

He thought about his, then shook his head. "Probably skunks or raccoons. Damn things'll eat anything. They'll crawl in bed with you if you let them." Michael jogged in place like he had to pee.

"C'mon," Oscar said thumping the mattress with his fist. "Hop in."

Michael jumped in bed next to his father and asked his father if skunks had long nails.

"Uh-huh," he replied lighting another cigarette. He put the cigarette in the ashtray and pulled one of the blankets over Michael. "Get some sleep."

***

He finishes taping up the last box and thinks about making breakfast for both of them. Michael is drawing at the kitchen table. He hides his sketches in a hat box he took from his mother's closet. Most of them are pictures of giant skunks in pools of pink water. After his mother died, he scribbled a picture of a naked woman bathing under a shower-head that looked like a mouth. He called it *Lady in Shower*.

"You hungry?" Oscar asks.

Michael smears the charcoal pencil with his fingertip and saliva.

"I was gonna fry some eggs and ham and toast."

"I'm not hungry."

"You need to eat something." Oscar lights another cigarette and opens a window. "Smells like a locked-up fruit cellar in here." Outside, their neighbor, Ms. Trent, is tearing up pieces of stale bread to feed pigeons. Ms. Trent is a skinny, African-American woman. She comes out in a bathrobe and slippers every morning at about eight o'clock to feed pigeons. They lock eyes for a moment. "I mean, you haven't eaten a lot in a while."

"I don't feel good."

"Stop whining. I don't wanna hear you whining." He walks over and looks at his son in the eyes, then puts his cigarette in the ashtray. "You look like a starving model."

Michael draws huge, dirty nails on the skunk in his sketch.

"Fine," Oscar says. He pulls out a beer from the refrigerator and storms into the bedroom.

He takes out a ratty pink nightgown and a fake fur hat from the closet and throws them on top of a box. Inside, the closet smells like a bath splash his wife used every night. The mixture of bath splash and beer makes his stomach turn.

***

He carries one of the boxes, nightgown, and fake fur hat to the backyard. He picks up a shovel lying against the side of the house and balances it on top of the box. There's no fence separating his and Ms. Trent's yard. There's a mound of bread next to her on the bench. She's feeding pigeons that aren't there.

"What you got there?"

"Old junk. Clothes. You know." Oscar puts down the box and stuffs his wife's nightgown under the lid.

"What you gonna do with all that?"

"Bury it, I guess." He raises the shovel like he's greeting her with it.

"You better keep an eye out. The grubs'll get it."

"Huh?"

"The grubs. They come from behind the hill. Probably winos or dead people or something. They dug up my yard when my husband, Harold, died, oh, almost ten years ago now. I see them out here sometimes."

"I didn't know you were married."

"Yup. He hung himself in that tree right there. He was a good man. I miss him. Had a lot of friends, too. He was a baker. The grocer still gives me free produce and stuff when I go in town."

"I'm sorry to hear."

"Me too."

Oscar rubs his face. He feels himself going numb. He gets to the topic. "But I don't think there's anybody out here except skunks and raccoons and stuff."

"Well, I didn't want whatever it was getting to Harold's things. I burned his clothes. I piled his underwear down in the valley and lit them on fire. They were just briefs, anyway."

He kicks the box and leans on the shovel. Michael is in the window looking at them. He looks more and more like his grandfather. Pale lips and brown skin. Oscar begins to sweat. It's about nine in the morning.

"Your boy's getting big, huh?"

He nods.

"And dark. He's good-looking. He's gonna be a warrior when he grows up. I can tell these things." She looks past Oscar. Michael puts his long, scrawny fingers up to the window. The pane steams up.

"My dad was half Mexican and half Apache Indian."

"Really. He's dark as Jesus."

"I dunno why he's getting so tall." Oscar clears his throat and changes the subject. "Ms. Trent, have you been having problems with skunks or raccoons at your place?"

She becomes aware that Oscar is still in front of her. "Why do you ask?"

"Well, you see, my son says he heard scratching at his window. Couple of nights in a row I found our garbage meddled with. I'm thinking it's skunks or raccoons. My son's afraid of them."

She points her index finger at him like a school teacher. "Them grubs, I'm telling you. Besides, you don't wanna go messing with skunks. You ever see the nails on those things?" She chews on another piece of bread. "You see all them baskets and things I have stacked in my kitchen? They're filled with tomatoes and heads of lettuce and garlic and some of Harold's dusty books. Garlic and dust is what keeps them away. They're like vampires."

Oscar feels his foot going to sleep. He fiddles with the shovel, nods his head, and makes a motion to pick up his box.

"You're finally gonna bury them things in the backyard, are you?"

"Nobody wants this stuff anymore."

"Well, you might give them to me. I bet your wife had some pretty things to wear. She was a beautiful woman, your wife was. It's a damn shame."

"She was pretty."

"I think they're probably too big, though. It's about time I gained some more weight, don't you think? I've lost forty pounds in the last ten years since Harold died."

He pushed the box toward her with his foot. He didn't care where those things went. He didn't want to look at them or pick up the box. His wife's perfume was all over them. "You keep it, I guess."

"I'll trade you something of Harold's I got left. Come out here again tomorrow morning and I'll give it to you."

***

"You *gave* away mom's clothes?"

Oscar locks the back door. He sees Ms. Trent putting nightgowns up to her chest as if she were in front of a department store mirror. "She's kinda crazy. Anyway, we don't need them laying around anymore."

"But they were mom's."

"Look, I've had enough of this. All right. We don't need them laying around. It ain't right."

Michael throws a bunch of his drawings on the floor and storms out of the room.

"Get your ass back here! Come pick up this shit!"

The bedroom door slams. Oscar massages the muscles in his neck and opens the refrigerator. He gets a beer and drinks it as fast as he can. He sits in the middle of the kitchen floor trying to remember his wife's face. He gathers four beers on the kitchen floor with him and opens them all. He almost cries because her voice is lost somewhere in his memory.

***

Oscar wakes up on the couch. It's evening, maybe six or seven. He's drunk and pissed, but can't remember why. "I can't wake up," he says to himself.

He staggers into the kitchen. Michael is sitting at the table playing with army men. "Blam! Blam!" he can hear his son say somewhere in the distance. It feels like his eyes are glazed over with Vaseline. Michael is blurry and he can see the movement of each of his arms as if in slow motion. Before he knows it, he's directly behind his son. He hears himself screaming. "Sit up! Your posture's fucking terrible!"

Michael freezes.

Oscar grabs him by the hair and pulls his head back slightly. "Open up." He picks up a plastic army man and puts it up to his son's mouth. "Make it go down. You're not gonna starve yourself to death. I'll feed you pincher bugs if I have to, goddamn it."

Michael swipes at his father's hand and knocks the toy to the ground, then screams in a high-pitched voice. Oscar is sobered by the image of his son screaming. Michael runs outside and Oscar's about to run after him, but counts to fifty in his head to slow himself down.

***

It's dark and he hasn't heard Michael come home, but Oscar is pleased. There's nothing in the house. Empty. He can barely make out the sweet perfume that seemed to be everywhere before. He's almost asleep on the couch again when he hears a scratching that sounds like nails against a chalkboard. He can't tell where it's coming from, but it sounds like it's coming from inside the walls. Immediately, he thinks it's a skunk. One broke into their house when his wife was still alive. It was trapped behind the stove. He gets a chill down his spine thinking of its tense, muscular body ready to attack or spray itself all over him.

He gets up and looks outside. Through a porch light, he can see that Ms. Trent left a mound of bread and shredded lettuce in the middle of her backyard. From the edges of the dim light, he sees the silhouette of a man. The man steps into the stream of light and

Oscar can see that it's a naked black man dressed only in white socks. He looks frail and dirty. His hair is caked with mud and leaves. The man goes through a box and shakes an old book to see if there are any scraps of paper stuck inside its pages. Dust rises into the porch light. Then he sits next to the pile of bread and begins to nibble on pieces.

Oscar runs into his bedroom forgetting about his son or his wife or dead people, suddenly sober. He opens several drawers and empties them onto the bed until he finds his Polaroid. He checks to see if there's any film. When he gets to the window, he sees that the man is flapping two broken branches and twirling around in the backyard. Oscar takes picture after picture, letting them fall to the ground until there's no film left.

He watches the man walk towards the edge of the light and down the hill until he can't see him anymore.

Oscar twirls around and the whole room spins. He forgets he's still drunk. Right then, he hears a "Hsss!" along with scuttling and scratching coming from his son's bedroom.

He opens the door and is immediately hit with a sour stench. "Who's there'?" He shakes and can't move for a moment, but manages to turn on the light. Michael is sitting on top of his laundry in the corner near an upside-down, wooden crate. Inside, he can see a skunk twitching back and forth. He's stunned. "You trap this thing?"

Michael looks as if he's meditating. He brings his hands up to his face, taking deep breaths of the skunk's odor.

"You sick little fucker! I'm gonna lock you up in a funny farm. You goddamn idiot!" He picks Michael up by his shirt, plops him down inside the kitchen pantry and barricades it with the china cabinet.

He goes back in the room. The skunk is nervous

inside the crate. It shakes and hisses. "Fucking piece of shit." He grabs a broken broom handle from under the sink and beats the skunk through the wooden crate until it stops moving.

***

By the time he sobers up, it's morning. The sun is peeking through the blinds. He's lying in the kitchen on top of the Polaroids, blood all over his khaki pants. He can hear somebody yelling his name from the backyard.

"Mr. Perez? You awake? I got something for you."

He peeks out the kitchen window. Ms. Trent is sitting on her wooden bench waving a loaf of sourdough bread. He closes his eyes for a second, then gathers all the Polaroids on the floor. He walks outside rubbing his stubble.

She's still waving and smiling until he gets close enough for her to smell him. Ms. Trent crimps her face. "What the hell happened to you? You smell awful."

Oscar rubs his face. "Ms. Trent, we had a skunk in our place last night. It smells like a slaughterhouse."

She laughs and throws bread onto the lawn while pinching her nose. "Well, I got something for you, Mr. Perez, since you gave me your wife's belongings and all."

"So do I, Ms. Trent. I have some pictures for you." He watches as she turns to him with solemn eyes. "I saw your husband last night. He was in your backyard. I swear. I have pictures."

He hands her the Polaroids and she glances at them with a half-expectant look, as if she might actually see her husband's face. She puts them down on the bench after a couple of minutes. She's shaking her head. "You need to take care of that stench and feed that boy of yours, Mr. Perez." She pulls a couple grocery bags from under the bench. "Here's some apricots and tomatoes they gave me at the grocer yesterday. They always give me free stuff. All I got left of Harold is his good name."

Oscar takes the bags in his arms like they were children.

"You wash yourself and your boy with tomato paste. That'll get the smell out, believe me. Boil them down and scrub them into you like it was soap. Any furniture that got sprayed, rub it into them, too." She grabs the Polaroids and puts them up to her chest. "God bless you, Mr. Perez."

Oscar boils them down. There's three huge boilers bubbling with thick tomato juice. He's almost gotten used to the odor. He thinks he should've burned all his wife's clothes and given his son up for adoption. What's he gonna do with a sick kid who doesn't want to eat? All he can see is tomato paste. Steam fills the room like food. Before he knows it, he's covering the floors, walls, couch, counter, and refrigerator with paste and seeds.

He sits on the floor, drinks from a warm can of beer and looks at the china cabinet in front of the pantry. He stands up, a little bit light-headed, and pushes the cabinet out of the way. Inside the pantry, Michael is balled up with his shirt over his knees. He picks him up ever so gently. Michael squeals—putting up a fight, at first—and kicks his father in the chest. Oscar is almost out of breath, but is able to keep walking with his son in his arms. He sets him down at the kitchen table near a pot filled with tomato paste. Oscar takes handfuls and begins rubbing it into his son's hair like shampoo. Michael opens his eyes, and before they know it, they're spreading handfuls on themselves.

THE AIR APARTMENT

It's hard to tell how many millions of cars. It's night, headlights are on, cars clamber toward the tollbooth. "Have a nice day," I say. "Have a good day." I take their money. A woman gives me a note along with the toll. She has glasses and a fat lip and asks for a receipt. As she drives off, I read her note. *Would you ever blow up this bridge?* I pin it up to my bulletin board then take it down, having decided I should turn it in to my boss. It's the proper thing.

My radio sounds. It's Lena's voice, but I can hardly make it out so I switch the channel. "Emissary Eighty-Four?" she says. I answer and tell her to call me Aster, but she insists on formality. We chat as we take toll. She started a couple of weeks before and is several booths away, I know that. When she started, I showed her my booth. "There's a proper décor," I said to her. I pointed out the photograph of my mother. My mother was twenty-two in the photo wearing a fine, curly wig, and eyebrows shaped like half-moons. Lena rubbed her chin the whole time, nodding. Pencils in good order, toll-log neat and without scrawl, no dust or mites. She was impressed. We've been lunching in the dining hall two to four times per week for several weeks now.

A man pulls up driving a sterling silver mobile. I think he has one violet eyeball. "Slow son of a bitch," he says throwing a bill at me. I straighten out the bill. On it is a message scrawled in purple ink: *Your bridge leads from Heaven to Hell!*

As the man zips toward his inevitable doom, I'm compelled to reach for my groin. As if my hands could protect them. As if I ever had a chance.

"Meet me in the dining hall, Emissary Eighty-Four," Lena says over the radio.

The dining hall is inside the bridge. We trek down the stairs into the fuzzy light and stay the appropriate distance from each other—my heart doing flips. We talk about the people we've encountered that day. She mentions some brooding teenage boy in a convertible. "He made an insulting remark with his finger to me," she says. I nod and say, "It happens." I can hear the hum-cycle of cars above me. There's the thump-thump as they go over the divides in the pavement.

"How about sitting over here?" I ask.

"Sounds blissful," she says.

I chuckle.

She sits across from me. She has already paled since I met her. Living inside the bridge will do that. Her apartment is in the Recruits In Training wing. My apartment is tucked away at the end of an L-shaped hall. When I go to bed thinking toll-takers' thoughts, I imagine I am actually in a submarine. I used to do this as a child. As I clocked away into drowsiness, my stomach would go loopy, and I flew places. That's the way it is now in my apartment at night. The cars go ad infinitum. The ocean is among us. The bridge, our home.

"What are you having?" I ask.

"Not sure," she says. She gives me a perplexed smile.

I turn away. Men must turn away in moments like these.

"What are you having?" she asks.

I tell her. She says she will have the same.

"Order for me," she says.

Our table is one of those that have a coffee spigot. It's basically a small, rubber hose that's connected to a barrel of coffee. The table is not really a table, but a solid cube of wood with a hole into which I give our order. "Dark coffees, two. Scrambled eggs, two orders. Simulated beef, also two orders," I say into the hole. I imagine there's a person inside the solid cube of wood, but there's probably just a microphone. Lena turns on the coffee spigot and puts my cup under the hose. Out comes a cultish liquid, and I am already agonizing because I've been experiencing withdrawal all morning. Our food comes. Lena gives me this purely gleeful smile. Her hair is perfect in the way lawns are perfect. I suddenly get a soft feeling. I imagine even her teeth are lined with transparent fur, she's so soft. A bit of coffee pools onto the table. My mind pictures both of us in a sea of coffee, making ruckus in a forest. What I'm actually imagining is a forest of sequoias submerged in an ocean of gourmet coffee, us creating babies. Everyone says the forest is an optimal place for nudity. "Your face is as soft as bread," I whisper to her.

She's about to put a forkful of simulated beef hash into her mouth. She blushes as I say this.

I wish I could retract it.

***

Someone knocks on my door. It's late. There's a moment of disorientation.

I look up toward the sound of cars passing above, look at my wiry hands. "Our wing is having a meeting," a guy says through my door. I put on a robe and walk out and see Old Surge. I don't know why they call him Old Surge. He's a lanky man, probably late in adulthood, and reminds me of a horse's head with a cowboy hat. He always wears a ten-gallon hat, even to bed, I think. He basically has a porcelain mantelpiece for dentures. They stick out like crazy.

"Something's amuck," Old Surge mutters through his teeth.

"Damn straight," another guy chimes in.

"What's it about?" I ask.

Old Surge swivels his gargantuan head. "Some kind of stirring-up in the new recruits' wing," he mutters.

Our wing director walks in gallantly. He's wearing shiny pants, a dress shirt, and even some kind of turtle pin on his collar. He looks to the ground for effect, shaking his head as if he is truly depressed. "Brethren," he says. "I have had a vision."

"Uh-huh!" the crowd chimes in.

Old Surge puts a toothpick in his mouth. "S.O.B is crookeder than a dirt road," he whispers into my ear.

I put my hands in my robe. Lena, in an ivory-colored gown, is regaling for the crowd. Men will bow to her. Her face is so moonstruck it's almost devastating.

"These days have brought forth not only semi-darkness, but a new light. A new light, I say, I repeat. Because I," he says motioning to my Lena. "We among us have THE WAY OUT," he says kissing Lena's hand. She seems to frown. We make eye contact and she shrugs. "I have had a vision and it is Lena... She is the one we've waited for to lead us from this way station..."

"Shit," says Old Surge, adjusting his ten-gallon hat. "Well maybe the som-bitch is right." Surge has a spellbound look and an aura. He puts his hat over his heart. "I see it now."

I watch Lena. She glances at me and waves. She is gorgeous. Absolutely. Mine, she was.

***

Things have been different. Although she's called me on the radio, I've sensed a slight change in her voice. I can't pinpoint it. We've met less frequently for simulated beef hash. The last time we met, she only had toast. "She really is the goddess, ain't she?" Old Surge asked.

Half-sized statues carved from soap line our corridors. Mostly white soap, but a few purple ones, too.

Tonight, we have a subdued gathering. Four

men raise Lena above their heads as she sits on a makeshift throne. We are heading toward above ground. The wing director—decked in leather pants and silk shirt—leads us with his head in a slump. We're about one-hundred-fifty or so. I'm in the middle of the procession following Lena on her throne. I can see the back of her head as it bobs up and down. Not all of the tenants have joined us. An older woman with her toll-taker uniform on peeks out from behind her apartment door and has a look of fright on her face. When we get to the outside, we gaze. The bridge has been closed. We look out at the still sea and the lights of the lands on each side of our bridge. All of us, yes, have yearned for knowing how it is out there. But I don't want her to be our goddess. I love her, but she is so distant.

  I kick around an apple core. I reach into my pocket and take out a wire-mesh figure I made in my room. I made it from copper. It's a representation of Lena. I spent a week twisting the wire, making arms, legs, and a head. I play with the copper-wire feet. People are getting roused, thumping the ground, and singing hymns. "Us believers!" the wing director exclaims. "We will be led!" I want to see the real Lena's face, but her back is to me. Her gown hangs over the edge of the throne. The men still hold her above their heads. I turn around and head back. People look at me like I'm crazy. "Excuse me," I say with a hint of despair in my voice.

  When I get home, I put the representation of Lena in this cardboard model of a house I made. I painted the cardboard house a peach offshoot. (I wish I had chosen a color more suitable to the life I've read about on land.) I made rickety chairs out of matchsticks. I spent a week or so fixing the sticks together with glue, then, when I ran out of glue, I took up chewing gum until it was stale. I put the representation of Lena onto the matchstick chair—move her arm to a position of waving—and try to make up dialogue.

I can hear them up there.

I also made this copper representation of a pet iguana. I always wanted a pet iguana as a child. (I don't imagine Lena is into reptiles, but I tell her in the quietest voice I know that what I love she too can learn to appreciate.) I put the representation of the iguana at the feet of copper Lena. "Oh lovely, dry, green skin of reptile," I make Lena say. I stop, though. I feel like this line of poetry that I uttered as a child is forced, especially in Lena's voice. I clear my throat. The crowds' chants above ground are muted and hushed by the massive thickness of concrete and steel. Their voices melt and wane and turn into one senseless word. "The crowd is destroying a love," copper Lena says to the iguana. I hang one of the miniature paintings that I made on the wall of the cardboard model of my house. I made a carpet for the house with glue and crushed cereal. *If I were to believe in God*, I tell copper Lena, *it would be an iguana, or some kind of reptile*. I put a piece of newspaper over the house to say *goodnight*. I lie on my cot, thinking. My hands are clasped over my chest as I close my eyes. The flying comes to my stomach. The bridge sways, I think. Perhaps the bridge is actually a submarine. I sleep and go wading in my childhood.

I have never left this bridge.

***

"Can I come in?" Lena asks.

I lift my head from my pillow and nod. My hair is matted and unkempt.

"You've been sick?"

I shrug my shoulders as I sit up.

"I brought you some food." She puts a tray on my bed. Scrambled eggs, dark coffee, simulated beef hash. I see the beef hash for what it is: brown and unnatural.

"I'm not hungry," I say.

"You should eat something."

The rustle of traffic above ground is getting to me.

"Can you at least get some toast down?" she asks.

I shake my head.

"Is it flu?"

A broken heart, I wanted to say.

"Have you seen the doctor?"

"No," I say. I look over to the model house. It's still covered with newspaper.

"No?" She sits at the foot of the bed. She smiles kind of dumbly, looks up, and walks her eyes along the ceiling. I wonder what she sees. "Maybe you need some air."

I don't breathe anymore, I want to tell her.

She chuckles. "When I was a kid, my dad used to put this ointment around my neck. I'd suck in the vapor. It had this strong, medicine smell. I didn't like being sick, but I liked that. I still like that smell. I don't know. It always made me feel better." She begins to nibble at my scrambled eggs. "You sure you don't want any?"

"Maybe I'll have some."

She reaches for my fork and scoops up some eggs. "Here ..."

"Maybe not," I say and lie back down.

She sits there. I can hear her thumping nervously at the floor with her foot. She begins to run her fingers through her hair as it rambles down to the bottom of her neck. I love that.

"What have they been saying?" I ask.

"Well, they want me to lead them off tomorrow, you know."

"Tomorrow?"

I wanted to ask: Will you come back?

She puts her hand on my foot, but lifts it after a few seconds and looks at her fingernails. "I don't know. I don't know why they think I can do this."

I want to tell her she'll never get off.

I sigh. My ceiling has begun to stain. There are globular marks on my ceiling the shape of little monsters.

She turns to me with that perplexed smile of hers. "Why do you think they think this of me?"

"They think you're a goddess ..."

She laughs. "Isn't it kind of stupid? I've actually been losing my theism, but sometimes," she whispers, "I still like to pray." She stands up and walks over to my portal in the wall. She stands before it. As she unlocks the portal door, she turns toward me looking for approval. She opens the thing and, on the other side, is a painting. I have never seen it before. The scenery is faded. It looks like oil, but probably acrylic. There's a dubious and dull sun above a poor rendition of a bridge. She sits back down on my bed and puts her hand on my thigh. We sit there for several minutes gazing at this scenery before she leaves me.

***

Above ground, it's quiet. There's very little fog and it's clearer than you'd think. The light posts are dozens of lined-up giant soldiers with heads smoldering white. I walk on the road instead of the pedestrian lane, against an occasional car. The people inside cannot see me. Cable is no support for an overpass like this.

This bridge connects nothing—there is no land, but only mind.

I have found the only way out. The edge of the bridge. I look to the blackness below and leap off. I learn to be insignificant, not a bomb, but a whole genus of raindrops. I am rain and I am mostly everywhere.

THE AIR APARTMENT

My lungs cast their net, dropping, dropping, and I manage a shriek that lasts. In order to contain this yelp, they'll have to renovate heaven. It goes beyond being heard. The bridge will know me, the cars will know me, the headlights. Faster I fall before I am falling. Please, men, build walls that can gather my body. Forget the bridge long enough to erect the house that falls with me. Why can't you imagine a staircase in thin air? And, even if you can't build it, don't you see I'm already descending? I pull the earth toward me. I'm a balcony collapsing. I'm the act of balding, each blubber is a hair that descends away from its source to the pillow. The waves below are more than firm. Sure, there's my mishap waiting at the bottom. Broken head and wrecked lungs, feet somewhere and splinters of me, no more posture. But if someone could simply freeze this falling, I could live here.

LOUISIANA

It was the year of the fires when I realized I absolutely needed my first love, Jasmine. Bigger than heaven she would become in the late stages of her cancer, but on the day I arrived at the Singleton mansion, she was glorious the way a perfectly groomed lawn is glorious. The front door opened and she stood—her face wrote with brooding and despair—as the glint of a smile fractured her expression. "Johnny," she whispered. She was in her nightgown and slippers. Reddish brown hair draped across her milky chest. I was already dreaming of her conical nipples as she welcomed me inside. We brushed against one another. I could smell frightful sleep on her from the night before—something akin to high-class perspiration. She was always one to dream about angst. Her hand was on the middle of my back. She said something, asked me questions. A painting of her great grandfather, Colonel Fester Singleton, hung aside the spiral staircase like a banshee against unwanted men. I stared at him for a moment, momentarily frightened.

She sat nervously cross-legged on the French couch. Her lacy nightdress just barely covered the triangle just beyond the thigh. I was glad.

"Have you come to win me back?" She was beautiful and already drunk on gin. The glass she drank from was as delicate as her white neck. "It's not a good time, Johnny."

I scooted closer to her. "You get married?"

She reached to comb the hair out of my eyes.

Her left, violet eye was fake and gorgeous. I had heard stories. I saw it clearly for the first time.

"I'm not married, Johnny. No..." She drained the last of the gin and cracked her neck.

I found my ludicrous hand on her thigh.

She looked at me. It was a peculiar stare. She was iridescent, perfumed, white, perspired, and depressed. She lifted my hand from her thigh. "Haven't you heard about us, Johnny? You've been gone a long time, you know." She twirled her hair. The bad eye had a life of its own. Part porcelain iris, part seahorse. "Our family's important again."

***

"Do you remember the petty rain dances?" I asked.

We were on the patio. I could smell fires approaching from the north. I put my hand over my eyes and saw tops of flames on the horizon.

"Oh, when we used to walk in our bare feet in the marshes?"

"Or, how about when we traipsed the backside of houses, playing burglar?"

"Are you shaking?" she asked.

I found my hand on her thigh once again.

"Did you know my mother was murdered when I was four years old?" I blurted out. I swept my hand from her damp leg. I sat on it, riddled with guilt.

"I'm sorry, Johnny." She slid her glass along the table, toward me. "Drink up, then."

I gulped the last ball of gin. It felt heavenly falling down my throat. "Me and my father were there. Those evil men took her outside and stabbed her with their bayonets." My face was red with heat, shame, and capillary sickness. "I don't know why I'm telling you this."

Her bony hand slipped over my crotch, then rested on my leg. "You were always able to tell me the truth."

"That's why I've had trouble with the females."

"You always seemed like your soul was

damaged..."

"And the sex thing! Forget it! I look at you now..."

She reached out and pulled my head toward her. We kissed. The sun was hot on our backs. It was afternoon. We were drinking. It smelled like horse manure and hay fever out there. I didn't know it then, but the fires were steadily approaching. "I've wanted you again for so long," I said.

"My life has changed, Johnny."

"You were always more beautiful when I remembered you."

"I got responsibilities..."

"You smell terribly sad and erotic."

"My parents died. I'm all alone..."

She rubbed my palm. My tongue was doing circles inside my mouth. Salivating, for sure. There was a hole where one of my molars should have been. My heart was leaping. I was alive. I was trapped. I was happy. My sweaty palm mingled with her palm. We looked into the distance. More gin was at hand. We didn't care anymore. Our love was so many childhoods away. She turned toward me and I was startled all over again by the spherical jewel in her socket passing for an eye. "Will you stay this time?"

"What do you mean?" I asked.

***

"You're not going to disappear?" she asked. We had gone back inside. She stood behind the bar, tongs in hand. She placed ice cubes into two glasses and walked out from behind the bar. I could smell her from where I was sitting: a mix of sweetness, classic soaps, and heat. The slip clung to her body—her triangle pelvis molded in satin. I had forgotten how brown and round her nipples were. Her face: gaunt and angular and strange. She handed me my glass of gin. "You won't, will you?"

I put my clumsy hand on her thigh. "No, my love," I said. I wished I could've retracted that.

I caught a glimpse of the fires on the horizon. Her front window framed the rows of distant, approaching flames. Miles away, perhaps, but I had begun to smell the incineration of things: hay, clapboard, shoe sole, leather, cod, home, swamp root, hair, and veil. "I wouldn't dream of leaving you now," I answered, as if to reassure her.

She sipped her gin, swiped hair away from her face. Her bad eye swam to the left ever so slightly.

I was horizontal on the couch. I stared up into the dome-like ceiling. I drifted for several minutes. It was hot, terrible really, and there was sweat everywhere. I imagined I was alone, but could smell a sweet body moving closer and bigger. I cramped my way into the crevice of the couch. I was making room for a second body. My heart was driving the car. There was fuel in the air. I had begun to see ash swirl in minor tornadoes outside. I imagined weightiness plumped on top of me, brown nipples and all. I could see right through her opaque slip. I saw and smelled everything. Her mouth went around my nose, slopping my face in a magnificent way. I put my palm on her rump and attempted to force her open. "Ah," she sighed slightly. My coat came off and the afternoon passed like that for a while.

But I must've passed out from all that gin.

I had just awoken. I looked up at her. She sat on a tall, antique chair I hadn't noticed before. She was nothing as trite as an angel. One of the chair's legs was slanted so that she was staring at me from an angle. The chair, so high, her head just barely missed the ceiling. Night was in the middle of its everything. A moon shone through her sheer drapes. Maybe we were under water! Yes, that was it! Perhaps it wasn't a room at all. She stared at me. Her hair and damp nightgown floated. She was a guardian. I thought I was safe.

That evening, I cherished every light beam full-heartedly. Stripes of red luminescence seemed to come from within the walls, from within her. My eyes tried to adjust to the burnished atmosphere. She wasn't on the throne anymore. I could smell her. It was as if all things—dresser, coat hanger, walls, bed, nightstand—were on a pond and in concert with some seasick machine. Her palm calmed my forehead. Hot the way dying was hot. I was levitating. "There, there," she said. Her hand down my pants! A great fragrance drifted sweet all over us—we were nude, for sure. There were two, three, and perhaps, seven of her hands on me—she was moving so quickly. She had put her face in the niche between my jaw and shoulder and breathed there. We were together. I was fumbling with her flesh, half not knowing what I was doing. The belt had come off. We were open. Her air was humid. A breast against my abdomen. The way I pictured her body in the dark, it was as if she had clones. Her mouth was strong. My hand in her thick hair. She might as well have swallowed the world.

Then, sleep.

I hallucinated. Her bad eye was comprised of several thousand gluten-based machines. It floated massively before me, swishing its optical nerve. Nothing existed except it and the dark. Through the pupil was its brain-center. I burped out, "Nuclear," sort of pitifully. There were eyes within eyes. It was the world to me. I played word games to stave off fear: bog breastbone blue fish death and buffoon. It stared darkly with its globe of eyes.

***

She led me by my right hand down a muddy slope. Vines hung from trees. The horizon, glowing with fires, looked like Jupiter. It was dusk. I fixated on the back of her sweaty head. Her hair draped down her back. We walked bare-footed. She was in her slip. Her buttocks shone through. I attempted to touch her damp back, but thought twice. "I'm sorry I left you before."

She stopped. "We're almost there." Jasmine turned around. She grabbed my other hand, and then hugged me. "Isn't this wonderful?" she asked.

I put my hand on her buttocks. "Yeah," I said.

"Remember when we were little?"

"I try not to think about it."

She leaned back slightly to see my face better. "Maybe that's your problem."

"What do you mean? It's just that it was all so painful," I said.

I stroked her back.

"You mean what happened between us? Or the rest of your childhood?"

A slight, flying animal swirled above our heads, chirping high-pitched music. However, my heart quickened as if I was unconsciously suspicious of the animal's intentions.

"Johnny," she said, shaking me lovingly. "You here with me?"

"Yeah, yeah."

It was a tiny bird, I could see. It couldn't have been bigger than half of my palm. The bird seemed to shimmer in the glowing light of the moon.

"I loved you, Jasmine," I whispered.

"I loved you, too." She rested her head on my shoulder.

The bird's music lilted past our ears, note by note.

"It's a rare bird," she whispered as if she had read my thoughts. Jasmine lifted her head to see it. I wanted to kiss her then. "Watch," she said.

Jasmine disengaged from me. I felt abandoned all over again. She reached her left hand into the air, summoning the bird. "Psst, psst," she uttered.

The tiny creature landed in her palm and seemed to fall immediately to sleep. "Have you ever seen anything so gorgeous?" she asked.

I petted it. It stood, eyes closed, beak slightly ajar. "My God," I said. "Look at its body."

"Cashmere blue!" she exclaimed. "Its body is covered in cashmere blue."

I petted it some more. How soft. Soft as the finest sweater. "It's beautiful," was all I could mutter.

She transferred it onto my palm. "From me to you."

I coddled the bird, and then put her in my shirt pocket. I took out a penlight. I shone the light into my pocket, hoping not to awaken her. "Jasmine, look," I said.

Her miniscule, phallic tongue peeked out sleepily from her beak.

Jasmine smiled and hugged me, careful not to hurt our creature. "Life can be so OK sometimes."

***

Jasmine and I had been something like lovers as children. There was nothing really physical. We were small. But I adored her. I know that now. I'd often watch her sleeping atop her grand bed in the middle of summer. She wore sweet, softly blue panties and a blouse over her flat chest. I could sit for hours watching her. She had an antique chair in her room—handed down from generation to generation—seemingly built for tall men. My feet hung over the edge of its velvet cushion. I felt like a prince. She always adorned a smile and swayed her eyes back and forth, quietly dreaming.

One day while she slept, I tiptoed out of her room. I must've been nearly nine then. I walked down the hallway, trying not to make the hardwood floors creak too loudly. I was somewhat frightened because she had told me of a distant relative who had hanged himself in a room down the way. She said his ghost lived in the hallways some nights, living off the hair her family shed onto carpets and bathroom basins. I passed a room with its door ajar. I peeked in and saw someone asleep under bed covers. I couldn't tell who it was. Its chest rose up and down. Next to it, on the nightstand, was a drinking glass filled with water. A violet eye floated in the glass.

I entered a small study. There was an oak desk near the window facing the marsh. Atop the desk was a phonograph with a conical speaker. I tiptoed in, my heart pumping. I knew I shouldn't have been there. As I approached the phonograph, I knew I would play the record. I cranked it and the record spun. I put the needle on and placed my ear near the speaker. A voice crackled.

"...the dead must be buried below sea level, for if they're not, they'll rise..."

The record skipped.

"State your name, sir," a distant voice commanded.

"Singleton, Fester."

"Rank."

"Colonel."

I wiped my forehead and looked at the darkening marsh outside.

"Do you understand the charges brought against you, sir?"

"Yes, I do," Singleton responded in a tired voice.

"You have been charged with murder and the sodomy of a child. Do you understand these crimes are punishable by court-marshal and death?"

"I understand what I have done, but they are not crimes," Singleton said more forcefully. "She was a succubus."

"Sir, you will only answer the questions

posed—"

The record skipped back to the beginning. "...the dead must be buried below sea level, for if they're not, they'll rise..."

***

Louisiana is a rest home for dead souls, north of everywhere and nothing, at a good angle.

To the lustful, inside and all places. To the ripped-off vernacular, the man who craps out Canterbury and glib poetry; to swamp rind, half-pious Grace, skeletons of the bog, worn prayers of a Duke for his maiden, hell hounds, the hag fish so close to God. For car wrecks, for rage, the silhouette in the window, for ghouls, and the debauched geniuses as well. To beauty and the benign, and to malignancy, to cancer, but most definitely to purple tulips. But never to ancestors, high-pitched birds, fire, and death.

***

"Oh, look," Jasmine said still holding my hand. "We've arrived."

It was a marsh—wet and overgrown. I could never identify birds well, but I thought I saw cranes. We had rolled up our pants, ankle deep in mud and water. We came to a hillside. We looked down on an open meadow. The sun was creeping its way below the horizon. Shadows glazed over the field. We walked down the hill. At the far end of the meadow was a cavern. There was a small patch—a circle—of charred grass and dirt. It took us nearly fifteen minutes to arrive at the mouth of the cavern and parched earth. "Look," Jasmine said nonchalantly.

There were three wounds in the ground that were, apparently, small volcanoes. I felt for my heart where the bird was. My hand lay over her. She was warm and still. I opened the lip of my shirt pocket and could still make out the fleshy tongue dangling loose. There was something terrifying about her. I could never pinpoint the source. But she was comforting. Jasmine and I sat near the circle of burn and were mesmerized by these small, volcanic mounds, no larger than anthills. Dark molten rock leaked out from the holes, occasionally burping out thin geysers of lava.

"There's nothing like this place, Johnny."

We leaned on each other, back to back, and watched the sun slowly descend below everything.

***

It was dark by that point, except for the moonlight. Tiny obsidian balls littered the earth immediately around the volcanoes. They looked like black pearls. Jasmine and I sat side-by-side. "C'mon," she said. We walked northward toward the edge of the meadow. Another hill sloped downward to a clearing. The grass was dry. "Sit here," Jasmine said. Three figures were illuminated by torches stamped into the ground, and medium-sized fire. It was much smokier there, from what I can remember, even though I think I had forgotten about the fires approaching from the horizon.

"Set her down there, boy," a man said. His body wavered in and out in the uneven light of the fires. "Tramp little girl, think you can get away from me..."

I tried to grasp Jasmine's hand, but she wasn't at my side anymore.

A boy dragged a tallish girl by a rope tied around her waist. It appeared that her hands and legs had been shackled. The boy pushed on the girl's shoulder to make her kneel down.

The man spat near her. "She done acted like a Negro, didn't she, boy?"

The girl writhed.

"Jasmine?" I whispered.

Smoke had begun to settle around us. Ash fell like gray snow.

"Colonel—" the girl blurted out.

"Shut up, wench. You wouldn't spread your legs for me so I could checks you?" He removed a musket from its sheath. "You don't wanna prove me wrong, then this boy here's gotta put you down."

The man handed the musket to the boy. I don't know how I heard it, but I remember the boy whispering, "I'm sorry, Jasmine."

Her muffled voice was like a high-pitched squeal.

The boy put the musket to the back of her head and a fist of light exploded through her face.

I twirled around violently. "Jasmine!" But she wasn't around. I was completely alone. I stood on my shaky legs—falling once, crushing that gorgeous creature as if it were a knot of twigs, and feeling as if my ghost sprung out of me—and ran the other way. Or, at least, I thought I had. My feet slashed through the mud until I came upon that pruned, loose-skinned old man in my path. He still had his military uniform on, but his pants were down and he was grabbing himself. "Where you running to, boy?"

The fires eventually incinerated the majority of our nested town.

***

I still see her sometimes. I'm an old man, but she's still young. I'll meet her near the parched earth and we'll sit, not talking about much, but just taking each other in. I've gotten in the habit of bringing wine instead of gin. We aren't kids anymore. One time, we'd gotten pretty drunk. I was stroking her neck. A swarm of birds circled over our heads. She had me flat on my back. Her face was as big as the sky and I wanted her to smother me, to take away my breath and kindly inject me with her smell. Her hair fell on my face. The planet was spinning on its axis. She lay next to me, and we laughed out loud, just laughed. A propeller-powered airplane flew over our meadow. It was nearly summer. I do remember, in shock really, that I kissed her right eye. "Jesus, Jasmine," I whispered. "There's nothing wrong with you."

She shushed me and grasped my frail hand like she had always done. "I dreamt you had died of cancer..." was one of the last things I spoke. Her slip rose past her pelvis, revealing her tummy and light-haired beauty. I think we were levitating. I really think we were. In a dumbfounded state, I blurted out, "Where are we, anyway?"

"Don't be silly," she answered. "We're in Louisiana."

EXTINGUISH THE LIGHT

"Why am I tied down?" I ask.

"Precautions," says the nurse. She has brittle, bureaucratic hair. The windows are painted black and there's a long curtain dividing the room in two. It feels like we're in a gym.

"Isn't this just a place for the homeless?"

"Homeless," she mutters. "It's more than that."

Gurneys and army cots litter the arena. A mess of dandruff, love letters, pens, and oil occupy the floor. From the corner of my eye, I see a woman masturbating.

"Is this a hospital?" I ask. My feet dangle off the edge. I try to move, but can't.

"Of course not." She's got a stomach that hangs over her waistband. She could be a belly dancer.

"Are you going to burn me alive, then?" I chuckle.

"Don't worry," she says, writing something in my chart. "It won't hurt at all."

***

If I could light this place on fire, I would. But I remember that fire doesn't work anymore. Electricity is scarce. When the streetlights do go on, the hedges look so foreign they might as well be couches. I'm tied down, but I get this childhood feeling that I'm flying. I remember that it's my duty to pay taxes, but the legislature has decreed that anything with my name on it should be banished. I'm becoming unholy lying here. A cash transaction in Arkansas begins a tornado in the middle of San Francisco. We haven't had weather in years.

***

The guy next to me wiggles in his restraints. His beard reaches the floor. I don't imagine he's colorless, but I can't tell where he's from. "It smells like armpits and chimneys in here," he says.

"Smells like ass," I say. "Are they really going to burn us up?"

He cackles. "If you ask too many questions, they'll fire you and you won't get your paycheck."

"Do I work here?" I have faint memories of assembling animals and watching them come alive.

"There you go again." The man yips and I'm reminded of my grandpa chipping away at trees with a butter knife so he could eat the sap.

"I keep thinking of flour," I say.

"Because flour is edible snow?"

"No. Because my mother made such wonderful things with flour. Breads, etc." I had forgotten that I was tied down. How could they lull me into submission? I don't need arms. I don't need legs. Boil them, for Christ's sake. "It was harmonious back then. It was as if nothing existed except hunger."

"Harmony is rationed now." He strains to lift his head and scopes out the room. "You're back at home," he whispers.

"But I'm not ready to be a child again."

"You know what I heard? I heard they create blackouts in the worst parts of the city to entice people to steal television sets and stab their grandmothers. It used to work. But now the people have organized into an army. And if you're not ready to be a child, they'll molest you first." He chuckles. "You should be careful," he says.

"Why?" I ask.

"Don't imitate my friends." He has the eyes of a social worker.

"Who are your friends?"

"I don't have any." I can see through his blanket that he has an erection.

"Then how am I imitating them?"

"By being you."

I look up into the weak, yellowish light of the arena. There are animals there, and trees without feelings. There is a man.

***

When I was a kid, Grandpa carried around a flashlight on this tool belt he called "speckled leather." My grandpa was a fireman and sat on the couch for hours in his uniform. In the dark, he placed the flashlight up to his head and made faces. He was tall and had pipes for arms. He lived in the ancient part of the country, near a cemetery where confederate soldiers were buried. *The faggot this, the faggot that,* he used to say. He was white and I was brown, but he didn't hold it against me. My nice little puppy, he called me. He said we were angels from the center of our deadly galaxy. He rubbed my stomach back before the police were invented. He smelled like eucalyptus and ash. There's a war without guns, he used to say.

"Can I get a soda, Grandpa?" I jumped up and down trying to touch the ceiling. A million tacks were pinned to the wall. They watched us.

"It'll keep you up." Headlights shined into our living room and cast shadows of him and me on the wall.

"I want to stay up so I can see the angels," I said. "What do they look like?"

"They look like you and me."

I frowned and pictured a mummy in a cavern looking up at forever with a patched eye and holding a rusted knife. His bandages unwound to reveal his insides.

I rubbed my thingy against Grandpa's leg. I

learned that from dogs.

He smiled.

"Can trees have sex?" I asked.

"Trees drop seeds."

I rubbed my thingy against his leg again. "Can I hurt people?"

"Too many questions will get you killed." A fire engine rushed past the house.

"Who'll kill me?"

He stabbed the recliner with his pen.

I placed my foot on this one brick of the fireplace I thought was homosexual. "How come we're here?"

He stood up and peeked through the drapes. The sun had begun to rise. "You see that other sun?" he asked. "Right there? That's where I'm from. I'm not actually here on Earth. You ever heard of holograms?"

I walked to him and put my arms around his leg. He grabbed my hand and led me into his bedroom. On his nightstand was an ashtray, dirty socks, and a hunting knife.

"I don't feel good, Grandpa." My jaw clenched.

"Now you gotta come to bed with me."

"Bed? What about the angels?" Every night, I was a mummy twirled up in bed sheets.

"They eat this time of night. I seen them in the fires I fought. They eat people with their eyes."

I started trembling. I hadn't meant to rub Grandpa's leg like that.

"Don't worry," Grandpa said. "The sheets'll protect you from me. But someday, you'll have to be tied down."

***

The guy on the cot next to me has fallen asleep. I stay awake by cramping my toes together.

They must've turned on the crematorium.

Nurses wheel people into it. My breath is going crazy. I'm trying to wiggle free, but I can't move. They're pushing men and women through the doorway, some of whom have had their heads strapped to the back of wheelchairs. Everywhere is full of shrieks. It's humid as a swamp. I can't describe the smell except that it's something between burnt wretch and hair.

And then, I see her. The girl. I can't get a good look, but she's like I remember. The straightest hair and gorgeous blanched skin. Hands like butterflies. Her unreachable tongue. She doesn't seem to have a face. I took it away from her.

"Is it because of her that I'm here?" I ask the nurse. She sits next to me thumbing through a thick book.

"We investigated that. There are no victims in cases like yours. There are only perpetrators." She pins her hair into a bun.

"Why is she here?"

"For her own misgivings."

"I want to say sorry to her. I want to give back her face."

"You're in no state to give apologies." The nurse looms over me with the fluorescent light glowing from behind her head.

***

Grandpa worked at an old firehouse in Kentucky. It was famous for a street lamp that had been on continuously since the firehouse opened in 1913. It was a proud brick building, fully Southern. The fire truck was an elegant monster. To me, it was a dinosaur that ate heat and flame with its hose. By night, the firemen sat on folding chairs near the lamp. They drank and smoked cigarettes and chatted. They never turned that light off and it never went out. Mosquitoes hovered over the lamp. Spirits carried their treasure to it. They were strong, foggy men. They were ageless and slept in their uniforms. Sometimes, in their sleep, they screamed at the light.

***

I recall the day when I first encountered the girl.

"Hey," I called out to her as I closed the front door to my house. "You didn't leave, did you?"

"I'm in here," she said from the living room. She sat on the couch with her back to me, watching television.

I walked over to her and found that she'd been waiting for me in a silk nighty and legs splayed in a V position. She swirled a glass of scotch and smirked. It was the beginning of the great consumption period.

I plopped down next to her. She was ethereal. Her skin was pasty white, ice cold and luxurious. I could see into her thoughts. I stuffed my face into the crevice between her neck and shoulder. She emitted whole pastures of sweat. "I dreamed of you on the ride home," I said.

"I want children..." She swept her bangs from her face.

I climbed onto her lap. "You sat on a makeshift raft. The town was flooded up to the roofs. A colony of rats circled around you. Not sure where I was..."

"Shit, what would I name the kid?" She gulped the last of her drink. "So, did I make it out alive?"

I pressed myself against her. She turned her head to the side and closed her eyes as I smothered kisses onto her neck. I hiked up her nighty. She didn't have any underwear and started undoing my pants. As I grabbed her throat and was about to get inside her, she opened her eyes from a stupor and muttered, "Oh, God, it's you again..."

Someone screamed in my bedroom.

I jumped up and ran in there. It was the same girl! Her hands had been tied to the headboard of my bed. Her beautiful straight hair hung over the side of the mattress. "Please, mister. I'll do anything you say. Just let me go." She tried to lift her sweaty head, but couldn't muster the energy.

"I don't understand. You're in the living room with me?" I quivered furiously. "Don't you remember?"

I turned around, but no one was in the living room. There wasn't even a couch or television.

"I'd dreamed of you. Remember?" I leapt onto the bed and climbed on top of her.

"Please..." she whispered. Her face was pressed against mine. "I'll do anything. Just don't hurt me."

"You said you wanted children." I squished her bottom jaw, trying to pry the hole open.

Both suns began to rise.

"Over there..." I pointed to the draped window with a swing of my head. "That second sun. That's where I'm from. I can think us to that place."

"Fucking Christ..." She squirmed and sweated. "Just take me back where you found me. Please, God."

I need something to eclipse the now, I had thought. Something huge needs to happen out in the world to dwarf my worst desires. "If not..." I muttered out loud. "I can't help doing bad things."

I ripped off her panties. She had a triangle down there. I was nervous. My right hand was shaky. "I loved you," I whispered into her ear. "I've loved all you girls."

***

"Can't feel my toes," I say to the nurse. "Can you loosen the restraints?" Looking to my side, I realize my neighbor had been taken away.

"I untied the restraints over an hour ago. Don't you remember?" She has this joyful eye that mangles my sense of being.

"I can't feel my tongue."

"That's why your speech is so slurred..."

"Are there doctors here?" I ask.

"Just to recycle the organs."

"Oh, shit! Am I dead? Is that what's going on? You're gonna donate my heart to someone else?"

"No," she says. "We only recycle the hands, feet, tongues, noses, heads, and eyes. Don't be so dramatic..."

She turns my gurney to where a technician in soiled overalls pushes limbs and other bloody lumps on a stainless steel cart.

All I can do is close my eyes, but the sight is branded onto my frontal lobe.

She wheels me into a dim corridor, past the crematorium from which I hear shrieking. The damned bitch is gonna go through with my demise. Her creamy fragrance lands on me. I look up through the ceiling. Each fluorescent tube of light is a scepter. One flickers as I roll under it.

I retreat into my head and can't hear anything any longer, blah, blah, blah. Nothing except memories.

I roll past my girl. Shit, I'm reaching out to her with my wimpy arm. "I'm sorry for annihilating you, baby." She's strapped to a dental chair. Her eyes track my movement. A dentist in a denim shirt pulls teeth from her mouth. She groans, her eyes in terrible distress. I try to say sorry again, but my vocal chords blow up or something. There's a stench at the end of the hall. Smells of incest or a creek that runs through a cemetery.

Grandpa. That demon-pronged coot!

An idiot succubus and vessel for everything deranged.

His heart deprives the worlds of oxygen and justice.

He plugs his sex through the meat of our race.

This is a coroner's office!
The girl is my invention!
She's prettier than a brick!

It's dark as shit all of a sudden. There's a rectangle of orange heat in front of me some yards away. It's a furnace. I know it's for me. It could easily melt iron and guts and bone. The floor has fallen away and the nurse has disappeared and I levitate two centimeters above my gurney. With the light growing, I see my restraints flapping around in zero gravity. Someone is huffing up ahead. A fireman in full gear has pulled out the metal tray from the furnace on which I will smolder and sleep. It's exorcism hot.

"It'll be awright," the fireman says from behind the shield of his helmet. "It ain't what you think, boy." He waves woolen hands toward the orange heat as if guiding an airplane to its destination. "We seen this thing all the time. It's gorgeous like." His shield fogs up from breathing. "They eat ya with their eyes."

I have no sensation. I am the victim. It's so funny because we're in Kentucky. The crackers, humps, mulattos, guns, wrecked soldiers, histories. It's all just a hallucination 'cause I'm sick with fever! Don't judge me for being a murderer. Don't judge me for telling you lies or being vague. Grandpa: that old thug. I wasn't born through him. I was patented by the oldest company of the thirteen colonies. I'm rammed into the heat. I'll raze this whole fucking dimension and stuff blankets into the mouths of schizophrenics to make them go ape shit. The firehouse's street lamp stands free in my mind's eye—brutal, sun-gorged, and attached to nothing except its own existence.

RECORDING A LIFE:
DATA TRANSFER SKINS

1. **"You need the 63-minute** reel with sync possibilities," the doctor said. "Approximately 15 reels per day. At the end of each day, you need a staff to sync the speech-recordings with life-events with a significance of magnitude 5 or greater."

2. Corridors A-N contain raw reels of the man's life-events. The synced material was transported along with the visual data, the smell record and the tactile transfer to the stockpile.

3. During the intake interview many years previous, the man said things like, "I think a wife would matter," and "I like filling my day with significant, pleasurable activities." The intake nurse asked if he could name a few activities. "Good food, a good woman and daughter, a spacious house, flowers. You get the picture?" Knowing that even a simple life contains too many nuances to record in full (not to mention that the man was already 28), she tapped her pencil against the clipboard in thought. "Have you ever heard of *regularization*?" she asked.

4. Contents of the living quarters: the high-backed chair, restraints, headrest, the view from the window, paintings on the wall opposite (e.g., portraits and a sailboat), a wooden table, the urine and fecal tubes, taxidermy (e.g., owl, cat, dog), and staff.

5. Components of the *data transfer skins*: speech socket, visual data device ("His facial expressions encompass about 50% of the genetic possibilities"), tactile transfer mechanism ("The pain sensor and the gradients of subjective distress are calibrated by primary colors and all their shades," the doctor said. "How about his pleasure?" a student asked. "Well," the doctor added, "it's my guess that *regularization* may limit the nuances of his experience, making it easier to record his subjectivity. Hence, black and white"), and the smell net ("Smell approximations, or the gases we assume enter him, are sampled once per 10 seconds from the perimeter of each nostril. Then, at the end of each day, an aggregate smell-experience is calculated from the data").

6. "No," the man said during intake. "What's *regularization*?" The intake nurse cleared her throat and paused for a moment. "For people who have chosen for complete storage of subjectivity, *regularization* is a means of restricting the number of life-experiences given during any day, making it easier to record a whole life. If there were too many life-experiences of magnitude 5 or more per day, there wouldn't be enough memory, right?" The man nodded. "Just think of *regularization* as a routine," she said. "A nice routine."

7. "It's organicity that's killing us!" the doctor exclaimed to a colleague in private.

8. The smell net, made of synthetic spider webs attached via pierces to each cheek. Gas molecules collect on the sensors of the net, keying data to the computer.

9. The man swiveled his head from side to side as they strapped him to the chair. His heartbeat picked up. "A portrait of an old lady," he noticed. "A stuffed owl, a table." There was a dead tree outside.

10. "I need to leave my mark," the man wrote in his journal on the last night he spent at home.

11. The speech socket fits like a gas mask around the mouth. It can record shouts, minute blurbs, whispers, and half-spoken words, all of which are transmitted to the computer.

12. "The body is the best vessel for data storage," the doctor said. "As long as it doesn't accumulate new experiences."

13. "I want people to feel what I felt," the man wrote in his journal. His home had three rooms and a daughter.

14. Thoughts of his daughter never made it to any data device.

15. It hears what he hears. No larger than a pinhead, the device is embedded along the inner cochineal linings. In lay terms, the device "eats up his sounds." The digestion of his hearing produces a white noise which he consistently notices as a "clicking tongue." (In various literatures, this is now referred to as "trans-gibberish.")

16. It is not possible to recreate taste simulations.

17. The strapped-hot resin against his *skin* from the restraints on the chair. His head that weighs. The smell net—its spider web as tenacious as a cloth of steel—around his nostrils and pierced into his cheeks. A speech socket—attached to the whirlpool tube—clamped against his mouth for recording what is now just hoarse blipping. ("Pussy, pussy," and "Species of larynx," and simply, "No.") The tactile transfer mechanism fits each appendage precisely. (The register of "burning sensations," "roaches under the *skin*," "roof nails through the gums," and "wetnesses," is high.) It has been 38 years since his *regularization* started. The eating up of his hearing never goes away and the clicking tongues have forever produced an experience that he described as "a crow raking away at my scalp."

18. Each device of the *data transfer skins* is a living organism, mostly grafting of the man's own *skin*. The speech socket and its whirlpool tube have been duplicated from a chafe of thigh. The tactile transfer mechanism (colloquially referred to as "hand and foot wombs") has been generated from drunkards' livers. The spider web of the smell net has melded with the other *skins*. And perhaps, the device as a whole has attempted sentience.

19. Other than the ornate cusswords the man continually uttered, the subject had begun to relive his own sentience as a kind of feedback loop. (The raw reels of the man's life-events show insignificant repeating of his name, like "Leland, Leland, Leland.")

20. The man began to have conversations with the *skins*.

21. The man eventually died. The date was erased from the data. It is believed to be in a leap year. The findings—a 38-year *regularization*—produced passable findings. The man's subjectivity, in the parameters set forth by the recording devices, had been documented in full.

22. Unintended effect of the data transfer: the *skins* (speech socket, tactile transfer mechanism, smell net, and the devices in the inner cochineal linings of the ears) are, in fact, alive. It has no appendages per se, but is a mold of a face, has a gouged-out hole and some light from deep inside its epidermis, the source of which has not been determined. Since the first *regularization*, what would be called the *skins*' mouth is an exact negative mold of the first subject. The *skins* are nourished by recording subjects' lives. When fitting its mouth space over a new subject—taking in the subjectivity of that person—it digests the data into soluble and passable inner data, sometimes referred to as "Leland-enzymes" or simply "moments."

THE BLUE DOT

I had every reason to commit suicide. I had absolutely no reason to feel guilty. Parents burned up in a fire many years ago. I had no children or wife. The woman I wooed last, Veronica Allen, rejected what I concluded to be "love." We had sex even though I was always disgusted by the act. Her breath was usually foul and a downer during intercourse. I've found this to be the case with most women. I was able to cum and would make her cum. But I swear to God when I splattered on her body, I may as well have shat on her. She said that she liked me, but I was a slowly sinking ship and she couldn't be "dragged down." She was beautiful (maybe not my ideal), had a gracious smile and way about her, had smarts, was a better person than me. She wanted "an adult" is what it came down to. She tried to keep in touch and "be friends," but it always seemed like she was flaunting her new men in my face. I would find out on the sly. I did a little stalking. I followed her and her new boyfriends. She never knew. So I changed my phone number and e-mail instead of offing the both of them. Ha, ha.

I pondered several options. It is cliché, but I wanted the least painful way out. I wanted to die without it seeming like I was dying. The whole point was not to suffer. The likely methods: overdose, being hit by moving vehicles, sliced arteries, gunshot, the open window or edge of a bridge.

I actually began thinking about it in earnest while teaching one day. I taught high school. I was never hip with the kids. They didn't hate me either. I would be the one they forgot. They daydreamed in my class; found it useful to write letters to their sexual partners. I never flunked anyone because I didn't want that responsibility. Later in life they simply erased me from their experience. It was a fall afternoon and the trees were dying. I sat on top of my desk and realized the holidays were approaching. I was alone, but I didn't give a fuck about that. I held a pencil in my hand and was about to jam it in my leg. I could tell the students were becoming restless. I pictured leaving the class-room without any announcement and walking into traffic. I knew I couldn't follow through with that specific plan, but the seed had been planted. My heart lightened because I knew then I simply needed a way out. That would get me through the day. I let the class go early, walked home and never went back to my job.

It was about a week after Veronica had left me.

I turned the stove on and put my hand right over the flame, but I couldn't keep it there. I beat myself up for that. I was weak. I got naked and went into the bathroom. The intuitive plan was to do something decisive. You have to get naked to be decisive. I sat on the toilet and looked at my flaccid self. How insignificant. I neither felt aroused nor repulsed. I had a box cutter in my hand, but didn't even make a gesture of cutting my wrist. I tucked it away in a drawer, tried to masturbate, watched television, and broke into Veronica's e-mail.

        TO: Veronica
        FROM: Jeb
        SUBJECT: Last Night
        Was so good to see U—let's get
        2gether again soon—J.

I got furious. Threw a glass at the wall. There was no catharsis. I just forgot the feeling although I had an erection. Having gotten enraged, the blood simultaneously rushed into my penis. I almost came on the carpet without any pleasure whatsoever. I looked out the window. Stood there. People walked past my house without noticing me naked. Just like always.

Veronica accused me of being "self-pitying." I told her I always seemed to get girlfriends who couldn't appreciate me for who I am. She said I was so serious. "You're too negative. How come you can't loosen up anymore? You had such a great sense of humor." Her breasts were always supple and snatchable when she was annoyed. I told her my previous lightheartedness was a ploy, my sense of humor a utility. It is necessary to be liked in order to be attached. These things had played out there usefulness, or else I just couldn't keep up the façade. She said she was so disappointed, but still loved me then. "I do love you," she said. It was two months before we broke up.

Veronica Allen she would be for the rest of her life.

I sat in a Starbucks unable to do much but pray and mock myself. I didn't have conversations for weeks and had actually forgotten how to initiate them. Looking out the window, I realized the parking meter in front of me was the center of the universe, but it was manmade. The parking meter's volume absorbed the coordinates of the universe's center, putting us in peril. I tensed. I looked around and saw a teenage girl's breasts as she bent over in front of the counter. Then someone parked and put money in the meter, but cursed because it was broken. "Expired," it blinked over and over.

Veronica is out there.

Veronica is a gargoyle of door-manned buildings.

"The girlfriend" became an abstraction, a hypothetical relationship. Idealized, despised.

So I went to her apartment and knocked on her door.

"What're you doing here?"

"To pleasure you," I said.

She closed the door slightly, her body blocking

the rest of the entrance. "It's not going to work."

"What isn't?"

"Well?" She shrugged, pointed to me, shrugged again.

"I don't get it."

"What's not to get?"

"So, you don't love me?" I asked.

"No, I'm sorry."

"What did I do?"

"It's not like that." She shifted her weight, looked down.

"Like what?"

"That's just an expression," she said.

"That's the problem with you. You never say what's on your mind."

Several minutes.

"You have someone in there?" I asked.

"No, but it's not really any of your business anymore. I'm sorry."

"You shouldn't refer to us as 'business.'"

"I have to go."

"Where are you going?"

"Inside."

"Literally or metaphorically?"

"Ah, both." Click of the door. Just like that.

Later, I landed on a website for sadomasochism. I perused the chat rooms and saw screen names like "bloody_glan280" and "orifice_death." I was sweaty, downed by insomnia and fungal toenails, and clicked on link after link. I fixated on a bulletin board and started planning my death. There were recipes for suicide potions, announcements for genital mutilation parties, and personal ads for slaves and zombies.

I was planning my own murder. I was still squeamish about actualizing my demise, so I wanted to form a construct through which someone with a masked sociopathy could test their abilities on me, the paying victim. I would leave the specifics to the killer.

It would happen within a prearranged timeframe in a semi-public area, but I wouldn't know where or when. I suggested several scenarios: car bomb, injection of poison while in a crowd, electrocution. But I was smitten of a sniper attack. I prayed for a budding assassin: sniper rifle with silencer. This, for whatever reason, was my preference. Murder me! Murder me!

A guy e-mailed me and said: "From now on, no e-mail. Call me at this number: ...from a payphone."

So I did and we spoke once. I agreed to pay him $10,000 up front and $10,000 after it was done. He used this mechanism that disguised his voice, so I knew he was professional. I sent a money order paid to "cash" to a post office box through which we would communicate further. After I was killed, my lawyer would deliver cash to a concierge at an undisclosed hotel. "For Elvis," my lawyer would say.

So transpired the uncomplicated plan. I was person A, he person B. I could not truthfully imagine his features, height, manner of dress, race. As I sat in a café, I fixated on a redhead interlocuting with a graying, middle-aged man. She reminded me of Veronica. The man's back was to me, so I constructed his face however I pleased. He was "haggard," I imagined, "high boned" and had "ghostly" eyes. This man was my killer. He sensed me through the back of his head. I did not stare at the head in fear of activating the head, killing me there and then. Even though I hired him to kill me, my defenses were triggered and I was scared. He stood up, turned around, and had completely clouded-over eyes and was missing half of his nose. He was blind. I was mistaken. Perhaps the redhead took pity on him. Anyway, they left and I sat there. I second-guessed my every move trying to brace for getting my head blown off.

I looked for him everywhere. On my neighborhood street, there's a Food Town I pass nearly every day on my way to the adult video bookstore. I concluded that the roof of the grocery store was the perfect vantage-point from which he could study me, engage me, kill me. I saw shapes, a shadow up there. I passed the store most afternoons at around 3:07 PM (at which time a young Indian woman usually swishes by me, "Excuse me, sir!"). On a day I forgot about my suicidal ideation, a projectile rushed in between the Indian woman and me. It collided with the concrete wall of a Chinese fast food restaurant, ricocheted, left a crater. He did it and he must have had a silencer! Where is he? And can you believe it? He missed! And I couldn't see anybody on top of rooftops nearby. "What was that?" the woman asked in a monotone voice. I said nothing, admired her hair and was about to ask her to join me for some Chinese fast food. "Did someone shoot at me?" she asked. I cleared my throat. We stared at each other. "For a moment," she said, touching my shoulder, "I wished it hit me."

I went back home and remembered having a small can of blue paint in my closet. I found it. Glanced at a merino wool sweater Veronica had given me. I went back to the wall and painted the edges of the crater blue. A blue dot.

I have acquired a particular form of paranoia which has nothing to do with the murderer. Women are very attracted to me. I can sit anywhere and women begin to leer.

"Fuck me!"

"Over here!"

"No, no, pick me!"

This is completely traumatizing to me. I have no capacity to respond. I'll look down and count tiles and if I happen to make eye contact, I'll laugh and ruin the possibility forever. I stare at breasts, of course, attracted, yes, but I'm about as natural as polyester! They're everywhere! They want me! And this is pushing me over the edge!

Upon waiting to be killed, I did a lot of

observing of couples. I was on the subway heading uptown to spy on Veronica once and was so fortunate to share company with a teenage couple. I was standing. They sat in front of me. The boy was scraggly and bearded (in a fashionable way), whereas the girl was typical in all ways, even having a pierced lip. "You could marry me and become an Israeli citizen," he said. "If we moved there, we'd have to serve in the military."

"I'm not fucking moving to Israel."

He leaned into her, smooched her face. He was forceful.

She stared at her hands. "In Germany, if you don't go to college, you have to go into the military."

He pondered. "In Italy, I think they make you go into the state police." He kissed her and she was getting annoyed.

"Stop smothering me!"

"C'mon." He nibbled her earlobe.

"Fucking stop it. I mean it." She pushed him away.

"I'll fuck you in the asshole and rip it apart so bad you'll love it—"

It was my stop. I got off.

I walked into the rain. Drizzle really, but so much wind. Wind is our peril. What perfect weather to be shot in the face. And where was he? It had been, what, two weeks since the shooting? I wasn't walking apprehensively. I think I actually accepted my fate, my hands in my coat pockets. I glanced up at Veronica's apartment window. There was a dim light. Nothing discernible. I didn't have any emotional reaction. You see, I wasn't depressed at all. I was close to being happy and I wanted to die! I went past the old stomping grounds and kept walking.

I reflected upon my life. I hadn't amounted to much. I was phobic, skinny, ashamed, wimpy, whiny, above average intelligence, but god-awful handsome. That was my biggest curse. I once had ideals, tried to be a Marxist-Leninist, but I no longer believed in anything, nor did I try and defend "the people" or "my race." Everything had become trivial except guns, bridges, and poison.

I walked and counted couples all night. I knew most were relatively unhappy. Perhaps love would've cured me at one point in my life. It's not even the inevitability that they would leave me in the end or that joylessness would return. I was simply fed up.

Then I found a girl online whom I chose to have coffee with. She was pretty hot. Black hair slicked back tightly. She was Latin, had onyx eyes. She was bright, but kind of "street"—she wore a necklace with her name dangling from it, *Elena*. She wore blue stud earrings.

I wore a black coat, Italian button-down shirt, black pants, slight hint of cologne. I'm not sure where I had found the gumption. I had learned to wear my hair messy.

We sat at a sidewalk café. I darted my eyes away because I just couldn't hold eye contact. *Damn, I'm such a pussy!* I thought. She held her head in her hands and I knew she was totally into me. "So," I said. The conversation had come to a lull.

"I want to be a nurse," she said.

A motorcycle sped by.

"What, I didn't hear the rest of what you said."

"I said my mother's a nurse's assistant."

I tilted my head to show interest. "They change adult diapers and stuff."

She looked down. I had said the wrong thing.

I'm not sure what effect I was going for, but I simply put my hands over hers and said, "Nah, baby, I just totally support your endeavor."

"But you don't even know me."

Her blackened tuna and salad arrived. Shortly thereafter, they brought my seafood tempura. It was quiet as we moved our food back-and-forth. "I don't really know what I'm doing," I said.

I smiled and she smiled back.

I was almost tearful. She accepted me. I was "a part of." My heart had begun to open. I looked down the street as we chatted and saw Veronica going into a subway station with another man. They were going to fuck later.

"Is something wrong?" she asked.

"You know, Elena, I feel there's always something wrong."

Then a blue Ford Taurus pulled up in front of the café and did what they call "a drive by." There was semi-automatic gunfire. Elena was killed instantly as a bullet struck her eye and the back of her head exploded on an Asian guy behind her. He threw up on his lap. A couple of others dropped to the ground, flopped like fish. I turned my head toward the car. The tinted windows were rolled up. My gaze did not waver. It sped off. The license plate was covered with duct tape.

I had set something in motion... In a dissociative, adrenaline-induced move, I took out a small notebook from my backpack and wrote:

I have a pouch made of skin. I wear it like a "fanny pack" into which I stuff my whole family. They were shrunk and I've had to arrange the hands, legs, heads, and extraneous parts into a tightly woven whole. A puzzle, really, but I think the best analogy is a rubber band ball where the teeny murdered meats sleep at the core.

Some of Elena's blood and scalp particles were on my face.

A young police detective approached me. I was still sitting at the table, Elena's body already covered. "I'm Detective Larry." He had an odd-shaped mole on his forehead that I tried not to stare at. He scribbled my answers on a notepad. And what happened? What sequence? Chronology? How long did you know her? Really, the first time? An Internet thing? Had you slept together? You know anybody who'd want to kill her? Know anything about an ex-husband? "Does anybody want to kill you?"

"Not externally," I answered.

He stopped writing. "Huh?"

"No persons, officer."

He stared at me for a sec, then gave me his business card. He took down my information. "Sorry about all this," he said. As he walked off, I saw him sneak a sip of soda from someone else's glass.

So I meandered uptown. Everything was grave. It was the first explicit, true and obvious sense of how one can "set something in motion" with unintended, immoral consequences.

You ever hear of a hip place for suicide? Not popular like the Golden Gate Bridge, but hip? I heard of one uptown. I believe I whistled as I walked. The brick apartment buildings on my left were nondescript, but there was something fluky about the electricity in the neighborhood—it flickered on and off. A couple of teenagers and an old man sat on a stoop, a paper bag in his hand.

There was a massive bang across the street just then as a body landed on a vintage Ford Mustang.

"Oh, shit!"

"Damn! What the fuck?"

A woman screamed out a window from above, "Those motherfuckers are at it again!"

"It's a jumper!"

A white man in a bloodied Italian suit lay wrecked on top of the car. The streetlights flickered out. He had a happy expression.

"Fucking-A." A scrawny teenager in a hooded sweatshirt walked toward the body. He walked slowly. No one else said a word.

There was a Lincoln Mercury parked on the northwest corner of the block. An obese man exited the car, heaved for breath, lit a cigarette. Under other circumstances, he would've attracted "harsh criticism," but he went unnoticed. He walked around the corner and into darkness. I had the thought, "It's him who's gonna off me!"

We stared at the body in silence. Kids yelped somewhere down the street. A husband cursed out his wife.

Then, after about fifteen minutes, the obese man barreled through the air. As he fell, the lights went on and off and he appeared stilled by strobes. He landed massively atop the other body.

The two of them made a weird sandwich.

Silence except for the slow wrenching of metal.

We walked toward the bodies as a crowd. "Motherfuckers," someone threatened.

"Stop killing yourselves in our neighborhood!" a mother yelled. "We've seen enough!"

Then a fur-coated woman landed on the ghoulish heap.

"Where they come from?" an old dude asked.

All of us looked up, afraid for what may come next.

We rifled through their pockets. The dead were the thieves. They had robbed us of our serenity and quietude. I got a couple of bucks and a condom off the rotund man. Someone ripped off the fur coat. We men had no trouble wading through the meat and the blood. Our hearts raced. I had a basketball game in my stomach. One guy even went to feel the woman up, but there was nothing left.

No sirens, no 911 calls, no police patrols.

People expired here. These dead deserved indignity and hatred. We ripped the bodies off the roof of the car, onto the pavement, dragged them to the other rubbish and broken furniture. Garbage trucks would come the following day. The teenager kicked the woman in the head. There was nothing else of theirs worth saving.

I got home. Scanned the area. I hadn't gotten rid of pictures of Veronica. There were frames at my bedside, atop the TV, table, nook. My obsession had gone subterranean at that point. I stripped naked. The café shooting was all over the TV. I thought he most likely would never kill me. I wanted simply to love Veronica, but the bath I heated was waiting for me.

In the bath, I was successful. There I lived and the water drowned. More soap, no human condition. I laughed at gravity. Paid homage to the drain, the pipes, to the outsides, the sewers, every place not myself. I heard a window open. Perhaps the assassin was with me in the water, invisible, devoid of body, pure intent. I was a void and a rag doll. I was a weak man. The water slowly drained and it was dirty with skin and my life went with it.

I had a dream about my parents that night. It was the only one I had in twenty years. It started with an "ampersand," then I was on a street I remember from another dream. I sensed the murderer was among us. Way down the street, I saw my father carrying a couch over his head with my mother lying on top of it. My father was barely there—pure "emotion." There was a crack house on my left. On my right was a pristine, titanium, windowless, doorless, seamless building. My father and mother were inside there by then. Great distress at that point. "Call 911," I told my sister who was invisible and living in some other part of my mind.

"Isn't that a little drastic?" she asked.

We had to get my mother out of there. A couch is no place to sleep on in the darkness in a windowless, doorless, airless, fearless cube of a home. As if titanium weren't enough.

"Just do it!" some disembodied voice screeched.

***

I was at another sidewalk café. I was trying to

get through a novel while sipping a cappuccino. My hair was rather greasy at that time, but was indicative of current fashion. Some police officers sat on the hood of their car a yard or so down. One was a shortish, attractive brown-haired woman. The other, a big fellow. They drank large coffees. I stood up and left my book on my seat because I was going to the bathroom. Never leave anything of consequence. As I entered the café, the cop car exploded. I was rocked to the ground, but was only grazed with some glass. I never thought I would see arms and legs positioned like that. I just sat down and watched the scene unfold, not in slow motion really, but in "casual time." People screamed.

The whole police force converged on this corner of the earth. Fire engines, ambulances, and later, uniformed men, the mayor. News people were let through eventually. A crew of detectives questioned witnesses. Victims covered their faces as they told their stories. Detective Larry—the one from Elena's murder—approached me. He wiped his mouth. "You again," he said.

"I suppose so." I had my right hand sort of stuffed down my pants, then took it out.

"You like sidewalk cafés."

"I guess I should stay away."

I knew he was thinking it was a rather strange coincidence. I told him what I saw, what I heard, where customers were positioned, what kind of cars drove by.

"I'd like you to come down..."

"Please, sir, I'm shook up." I paused. "I just want to pass out."

"Give me your ID."

I gave it to him. He furrowed his brow. "You're Elvis. That's your first name?" He was suspicious of me. He had it in for me. He had a reddish thick beard that didn't match his black hair at all. A hired murderer and Detective Larry were after me. Either one would do.

He gave me my ID. "I'll be in touch very soon," he said as he stared into my eyes.

"Yes, sir." I walked away, but turned around one more time. He had not let go of his gaze.

I got on a bus to go back across town. It is much more pleasant to ride the bus than the subway. It was half full. Toward the front, I saw Veronica reading intently. I couldn't discern the title. She was absorbed, more beautiful than ever. I didn't feel the need to approach her. My heart raced. I simply wanted to keep track of her. I lowered my head so she wouldn't see me. True, I wished she would never leave my sight. She stood up and read as she walked off the bus. She walked into a grocery store as we drove on.

An old and young woman sat in front of me. The older one had bones made of sugar glass, yellow-tinged hair, a face that was falling in on itself. She leaned her head on the shoulder of the younger black woman. She was obviously a health aid. The aid had her arm around her older patient. At first, I was disgusted. I had come to despise old people. The black woman had seamless smooth skin. There was stillness. The old lady barely breathed as the aid gave her the slightest kiss on the forehead. It was the most important moment of my life.

I saw him when I looked out the window. My head was in a daze. He was in the driver's seat of a blue Taurus wearing a Richard Nixon mask, pointing a revolver at me. I couldn't believe no one else saw him. I pointed to myself and shrugged, "Why not?" He didn't move. As the light turned green and he sped away, I knew he wouldn't do the job I hired him to.

I got off the bus fifteen or so minutes later. As I walked across the street, a blue Taurus barreled toward me. I froze and had no emotion. At the last second, I jumped out of the away and the car passed frightfully. I was lying on the sidewalk. "Oh my God!"

"You all right, pal?"

"Did someone get the license plate?"

I missed my only chance.

If only I were a bodiless head with arteries and veins rooting into specially made vitamin ooze. Veronica turns off my nerves. My head is above ground in a hydroponic moss—oxygenated, fragrant, comforting, green. Breezes on my face pass for time. Time flies. At first, there would be "phantom limbs," but Veronica eliminates my "body memories," and I am fine. With an amputated spirit, I'd lose my ability to love, but I "remember." I'd want hypothetical caresses, but would not "yearn." In the end, I would still have to depend on the humans...

I was in the bathtub when the police knocked on my door. "Yes," I answered. Detective Larry and a couple of other cops were there and, after I put on some pants and my shoes, took me "down to the station." They interrogated me. "We identified the owner of the blue Taurus." They tracked it to an elderly Chinese woman. They found her head in her freezer. No fingerprints in the rest of the apartment other than hers. She had no children, wasn't close to any of her neighbors. But the police found an envelope under her mattress with $5,000. On it, someone had written my last name in block letters. Detective Larry recognized my name.

I sat at a table in a stuffy room at the police station. An older detective with a clean-shaven face, baldhead and a "scrunched up look" simply stared at me from across the table. Then he leaned back and plopped his feet onto the table. He sipped a diet Pepsi. It was all rather unnerving.

"How you involved, Sunt?"

"I'm not. I swear to God."

"You can't deny it's kinda weird to find your name on that envelope."

"Nothing conclusive." I cleared my throat. There was a bowling trophy on top of a filing cabinet to my right. "Just loose strings."

"Strings," the detective repeated. Detective Larry came in, took off his jacket, rolled up his sleeves. "You're involved, all right." He tapped his front teeth with his finger for some reason. "We got a thumb print off one of the bills."

"You hire someone to kill them people... Elvis?" the other one asked as he stared at my ID. "Fucking shit. You're the king? You the king, sick fuck?"

"Who is it?" Detective Larry asked.

"Why'd you do it?"

"Tell us right fucking now."

I simply shook my head.

"Where's the rest of the Chinese lady's body?"

"You rape her?"

"You sick fuck," the older one exclaimed.

Detective Larry slammed his fist on the table.

"What is it?" the older one said in a low voice. He lit a cigar, his feet still propped up. "You don't have a purpose in life? Got a beef against these people, got nothing better to do? I've seen sick fucks like you my whole goddamned career. You need some kinda philosophies, but you're weak. So, you get a partner? That's the lame ass shit... can't even do it yourself."

"We lost two of our own," the other detective said.

"Blown to fuck."

"No one knows you're here."

"A jury trial doesn't really mean shit to us."

"And that little Latin girl was so cute, man."

"We could do a lie detector..."

I put my hands on my face and began to yell, "OK! OK! I did it, but I hired this guy to kill me! I don't have anything to do with these murders. At first, I thought they were mistakes, you know? He missed? But then I got it he was playing with me."

The older one sipped his diet Pepsi, then broke into a laugh, ha-ha-ha-ha-ha, just like a semi-automatic gun. He sipped the cola again, but started laughing so it spewed from his nostrils. "Shit... that's the most ridiculous thing I ever heard!"

"I wouldn't have had the guts to off myself, sir."

Detective Larry took his gun out of his holster and pointed it at my head. "You got a death wish? I could put your brains all over this county. Ain't no other cops looking in here right now. I could put this gun in your mouth, you sick fuck, and it would feel just like a cock in there except a little more metallic."

There was a knock at the door and a female detective came in, got up to Detective Larry's ear and whispered. He laughed. "They just got a big old palm print of yours off the blue Taurus. The only print. We never had any print on the bills."

"Never," the other one chimed in.

"That blasted car nearly hit me! I jumped out of the way and must've grazed against it somehow!"

"A whole fucking clear distinct palm print? You're juice for the game... king."

Detective Larry just closed his eyes standing up.

The older one propped his feet on the table. "Sick fucking fuck."

In part of a book I was reading, the writer alluded to an experiment: some researcher puts chimps in concrete, seamless cubes. Their faces press against tiny slats on the door. Their eyes, the world. They go crazy and most of the chimps end up chewing themselves to bits. But then you put a hole in the wall that leads to a bottomless pit. The chimps stare out the hole, go back into the opposite corner, pick at themselves, go back to the hole, just about jump out, but get down. They are able to sleep. Anxiety lessens ever so much.

And so they took me downstairs. Detective Larry had his shirt off and guided me by the elbow. Two buffed uniformed cops walked on either side of me. We passed level by level. "Hey, sick fuck, what you fucking now?!" That was a bosomy brunette unif- ormed, hair ponied, hand on the revolver. I loved her in passing and will always remember her: she actually closed her eyes and kissed the air. For whatever reason, the cops on that floor laughed.

We were getting into danker areas. We passed through a cellar of sorts where mostly older black men worked—opening boxes, storing things, lifting. "Gentlemen," one worker said.

And another stairway, a huge steel gate, piss- blanched smells. "He ain't shitting yet?" one of the uniforms asked.

"He will be," Detective Larry said.

And we turned a corner, into a cubed, seamless cell. No bench, portal, window, shithole, nothing. They planned to seal me in there. Mortar, brick, sand. Some of the black workers came down. One worker handed Detective Larry a beer. "He ain't worth a shit. You see, we ain't taking no fucking chance with the courts. And fuck, no one knows you're here. You'll be disappeared."

They threw me in the corner and I relented to fate. Complete, austere darkness, alone with the self smelling the self. One of the workers started mixing the mortar, getting ready. "Hey, you're gonna seal me in, right? It's been done before. You think you thought of this ending? Ha! It's not original at all!"

One of the workers spat at me. "Shut the fuck up before I rape you." They all guffawed. Ha, ha! These were evil men. "It's not about justice," Detective Larry said. "We like killing people like you." Then, the brick and the mortar.

It was obesely dark for a very long time during my life.

Food was spat in through a tube at one of the rubbed-raw corners. Air crapped out from a sub-tube. I masturbated in the corner across. Gruel, somebody's chew. Food as torture. I "ate it" smilingly, viciously.

Did I fail? They surely won't keep me here

forever in some sealed up cube under the cellar in a police station. Come on! That's totally loony. But did I fail? Of course I did. They conflated this assassin's "misfires" with my intention to die. I simply could not do it myself. I mean, how come the cops aren't out there fucking that guy? Well, maybe they are since I'm down here and can't really tell what's going on, but I surely doubt it. I know them by now. That killer is a real person. They have it wrong. He is not a symbol or extension of me. I hired a specific man who is as different from me as a man can be from any another man. They'll let me out. I will become undisappeared. There will be a trial. The two of us "killers" will be shackled together like criminals. "Suicide A, Murder B." Dragged up the court steps through a sea of cameras, questions, microphones, journalistic ambition, dress shoes, cell phones, virtuous women, the enthusiast about to write his biggest story and the man so incredibly bored reporting on crime, much less "regular life."

     I've begun to dig through the floor. It's so soft, it's meant to be dug through. There is a very deep place under me. Of course, it's just an under-architecture in New York in whatever station I have been sheltered. The sewage pipes, rat pilings, palettes. But I know there's a piercing blue light down there. I can't explain it. When the hole opens for real, I will see this blue light and it will flitter and I'll plummet toward it to my death. It's been planned all along! This thought is how I've slept all of these nights. I have a new suicide pact. It's obvious now.

SHELTER

In a very small house lives half of a man. He has one head, thirty-two teeth, one well-fitted suit, two legs and two arms, a head-formed plastic bag, two feet, one heart that is linked to his one brain, two perfectly blonde eyes, ten fingernails, ten toenails, two kneecaps and two knees, a large and small intestine (the pancreas excised, excised, excised), an inny belly button, one pulpy tongue, a larynx, a carbuncle, sinuses, one wart, etc., but has no fingerprints, no knuckles, very few scars and no birth certificate, no eyelashes, three-quarters of one stomach and someone else's liver, no pen, very little sweat but many odors, no ankles, no wrists, no voice, no shoes, only two dying and brown thoughts (one of which is "Anything can change your life"), no music, no pillow, no bed, no electricity, but one human. That is all that is left.

SAVA GEAN ESTH ESIA

The point is to strip down, get protestant, then even more naked. Walk over scorched bricks to find your own soul. Your heart is a searching dog in the rubble.

—Barry Hannah

The Abode

I drink coffee with Dad every morning because it enlivens my corpse. There's nothing like caffeine to make my lust perk up. Dad wears a fedora properly on his head every goddamned day, even if there's not a funeral to go to. Most mornings, he pays little attention to me sitting across the table from him. I've begun to get wrinkles on my face. Dad reads the newspaper. Sometimes, I think he's scanning it with his eyes unfocused so he can reflect on his humble and troubled life. I bet he's an introvert philosopher. He secretly thinks about the meaninglessness of life and why my mother had to die giving birth to me.

Our apartment is small and a little cramped, but it's neat because Dad has pride. He's always cleaning up after me, tossing my dirty socks into the hamper and putting my loose change in a porcelain bowl my mother brought from her homeland. Today, he seems to be focusing on worldly news—about the wars our country has plopped our daring little combatants into. I'm not a daring man at all. In fact, I don't like leaving the apartment much. I do watch the liberal channel because it puts me at ease that I may have a moral compass. However, I do not. I can't tell if I'm truly a rapist waiting to jump out of my skin. I sit across the table from Dad and gulp the coffee down as if it were holy water. I don't believe in religion, even though Dad is devout and idolizes the ridiculous pope. I wonder about Dad's head and what swirls around under that hat of his. He's not an enigma. He's just quiet and feels sorry for me. There are plenty of reasons for that: I have no woman to speak of (except for Aida the prostitute who spoons me several times per year) and that I'm getting older with nothing to show for it. Maybe not old compared to him, but old compared to most non-degenerates—maybe unaccomplished is the best descriptor. I suppose I'm not an ideal son.

"Do you want more coffee?" he asks in accented English. He's been in this country long enough, but he hasn't shed the throatiness of his old language. I know nothing about his native tongue or his heritage or the name of his home town. I guess I don't really care. I'm just an unshaven hermit watching cable television and the same news stories over and over. I do believe that our president is a tyrant by nature, but I suppose I am, too. I haven't told you about that yet. But Dad, he's got the Holy Spirit in his back pocket for easy access. You never know when you're going to need a miracle.

"Yeah, Dad, I'll have some more coffee." He pours it for me because he does pretty much everything for me. Sure, he can't shit or piss for me, but I think he would if he could. I'm his only offspring and I will die in this house, probably before him. He'll be alone, then. He'll have nothing to live for except swallowing bland nutrients, scanning the news and not absorbing a thing, walking about the park like some zombie and staring into the mirror—not recognizing himself.

He's stopped asking me a long time ago if I'm going to look for a job. I'm unemployable. I have a strange, inexplicable disease. I've been on disability for most of my adult life. He arranged the government benefits for me when I turned my insides out. He wasn't pleased to observe his only child transform into hamburger ready for the gurney. I used to feel like hospitals were respites, but I know now they're just for triage. They propel you back into your bloody life that's circumscribed by the walls and ceilings and floors of a dumb shelter. My life isn't meant for a mortgage or anything like that. I don't even know what that is. I get my disability check and try to make it last. I give a few bucks to Dad to show I'm a little bit less deplorable than a dope fiend. I quit the drinking gig several years back, but I inhale a good cig every now and then to give me a four-second jolt. Dad doesn't approve of my smoking (I can tell this from his wrinkled forehead when I exhale carbon monoxide into his abode), but then again he keeps his lips pursed and doesn't scold me. There are plenty of secrets between us, even though we know each other enormously.

"You like the coffee this morning?" he asks.

"Yeah, Dad, you always make it good and strong." I live for these morning rituals. Dad is a good soul, even if he deludes himself about the afterlife. I guess we all need something to look forward to, except for me. Especially when I was twelve and Dad found me unconscious in the basement with the ligature marks around my throat after he frantically unwove the rope. Damn, that lunging-for-the-end was quite exhilarating. One can get addicted to comas. Dad had to go and get the paramedics to resuscitate me. I guess you don't know that compartment inside me, but you will. I do feel shitty that Dad found his offspring doubled-up and ready for Hell, but what's a broken little boy going to do? I've always fantasized about sharpened blades, cliffs, fast-moving subway trains, broken glass, guillotines, the firing squad, and death row. They appear inside my eyelids like a silent movie. The grand yearning for annihilation invaded my head at the onset of puberty like a soothing museum of taxidermy instead of libido. Maybe there is a link between a boy's terminal lust and his death-wish. But I think I am the way I am because my mother died giving birth to me. Squeezing through the tiny vaginal opening or perhaps being purged from a deformed uterus perforated my emotional well-being and made me the way I am. I don't blame her. I blame her tiny vaginal opening and deformed uterus. From what I can gather, she was once rambunctious and a stalwart and dwarfed tyrant. But Dad loved her more than the sky. Her spirit was deeply red—the hottest of colors. But I guess a red spirit couldn't save her from her vaginal opening being too small, or whatever goes wrong during those labor mishaps. Maybe she hated me from the outset of my conception and could sense what I would become and just gave up in the middle of childbirth. Perhaps there is an existential link between giving birth and unintentional suicide. My mother's name was Elena. Maybe Elena just succumbed to the reality of having a diseased offspring, like yours truly. Elena must've really hated the idea of me. Anything can happen in this world. But I can't die when I will give birth. I have yet to find my own vaginal opening.

"Do you want to go to the park with me?" Dad asks as I lie on the couch sampling some powdered doughnuts. My socks are filthy. I think I've worn them three days in a row. It's not like I don't have clean ones. Dad does my laundry once per week. I guess I've just gotten used to the smell of my feet. Something about it comforts me, the way the stink of death comforts a medical examiner.

"Maybe," I respond with no intention of leaving the couch. I'm watching the news and they're talking about how conservative people are dumb and probably illiterate. I'm not sure that's true. You just have to pick sides in life. I haven't really picked any side, it's just that the liberal channel has a pretty woman as the anchor. Sometimes, I believe in the public good, even though I haven't had much chance to inhabit anything like a public. I inhabit my cranium. Even my liver is lonely. I should pay more attention to my liver and my other organs. They need loving, too. I'm an astronaut in my own land. I'm quickly floating toward Andromeda.

My name is D, by the way. Dad isn't the hippy-type to give ludicrous names to his only child. He told me that *Double* was the first word that popped up in the dictionary when he haphazardly flipped through it. He had just entered the commune of widowers and he didn't have the energy to give my name much thought.

His wife was dead in the grave. It would never matter what anyone called me.

"Well, I'm going to the park." He goes there to meet up with Lydia, the slightly attractive old woman from another continent. They dabble in personal histories. Truly, after about three minutes, I don't know what one could divulge about oneself.

Except that God himself did speak to me in the basement once, below *my* rafters, when I was twelve-years-old before the attempt, but I didn't believe anything he said. He was a Neanderthal with a protruding forehead and way too much body hair. Why the hell was he naked? But he did speak all the languages of the world, including the ones amoebas were inventing and siphoning from algae and the muck of the swamp. I don't remember exactly what God was exhorting, except that it was obvious he was lying through his yellowed teeth. I think he was trying to insist I *existed*, even though he may have been a figment of someone else's daydream. I mean, wars have been waged and people have been burned for this Neanderthal. I guess most people, especially children, who have visions of God end up on a committed spiritual path, or straight for the quiet room. I became despondent, blocked out God's perfect English, and retreated into my hermetically-sealed head. If God is a savage, I don't want anything to do with him and his animal-skin heaven. I decided, then, to dismiss the vision as some mysterious bacteriological infection that had mainlined heaven into me. I was terrified, as well as absolutely despairing, because the most important experience in my life was a lie and truly, truly unacceptable. I would remain unmoored until the end.

"I guess I'm going to the park, then," Dad says. I don't respond. The damned powdered doughnuts are so good this morning. "D," he says with a perturbed look on his face. "Don't leave the house without writing me a note."

I'm truly touched. Jesus, for some reason, he actually loves me. Him and his notes! "OK, Dad, I'll leave a note. I'm probably just going to lay here and then go into my bedroom and try to be a visionary artist."

He smiles, but then he frowns, because our lives are headed straight for a poor person's morgue. I wouldn't dare explain this truism to him. He still has a life-force to speak of, a journey to explore, although it's just to the park and to Lydia. I just don't have the gumption to explain the philosophy of the slab—especially after my twelve year-old boy experiment and the ligature marks on my throat and the grand resuscitation. It would break his aging heart. Philosophy breaks all of our hearts.

I turn off the television for no good reason and stare at the blank screen. It, too, has an expression. We don't have one of those high-definition gadgets, just basically a wooden box with an electrical plug. Its expression isn't generic like you'd think. It's deadened as if it were my despondent companion. I'm sorry for all of this sitting around, my friend.

Desire and the Umbilical Cord

I lie on my unmade bed. Damn, I have to change my sheets. My blinds are open, at least. I have a good view into other people's apartments. Across the way are fine-art condominiums for people with bright futures and futuristic refrigerators. For some reason, those residents don't care about the invasion of their privacy. They welcome it. It's not like here, with mostly old men, immigrant families, and chain-smoking quitters. Over there are young hipsters with no roommates to speak of, professionals with legitimate degrees and truly handsome people. It's part of their lease agreement.

The other night, I noticed a new woman in the condo, though. Her hair hung listlessly to her waist. She mostly comes home in business attire because she probably trades stocks or orders around men older than her. Maybe she left her husband. Perhaps he raised his fist at her and she pulled a pistol on the fuck. Maybe she left her life behind forever and changed her identity. I really like her. I can tell she would be an empathetic listener even for a non-talker like me. She would bring me out of my cranium. She would make my neurotransmitters nimble and alive. Serotonin has a way of making the paint on the walls brighter. I've given her the name Elena, after my mom. That sounds a bit disgusting, maybe even incestuous. It's not like I'm totally in love with Elena II. Her spirit is simply alive on her olive-colored face. She's, perhaps, from an exotic land. I want to hear Elena II's gentle voice. So, I've been peeking into her apartment for the last week or so. I haven't liked a woman since Aida the prostitute. Aida is a professional companion for forty-five minutes, almost like a therapist. It beats psychoanalysis. But Aida's different. Aida never thinks of me when she goes home, I know it. I'm a ghost in her hooker consciousness. But Elena II is someone else altogether. I bet you she wouldn't die during childbirth. She wouldn't hate me for being me. An intake nurse told me when I was twelve and, unfortunately, had been resuscitated, that I didn't have a broken brain, I just had a damaged soul. It was a nice gesture on his part. People try to say the right thing, especially for deformed children. But he was wrong about me. And he was bald.

Elena II usually undresses, bares her ample breasts and brown nipples, strips down to her panties. I'm glad this municipality doesn't close its blinds anymore. Everyone's a voyeur. It's like a new public health directive. As you can imagine, my body always becomes deeply interested when I see her in her natural state. I haven't felt this way about a non-paid woman in a millennium or two. It's surreal, really, because I hear her voice in my cranium. "It's going to be OK, D," she says in the way polite zombies speak. "I'm here for you forever and ever." She usually prances around her home, messes with some papers on her kitchen table, and when she goes out of view for a second and I get anxious, she eventually comes back in an expensive robe. It's like we're sharing a virtual home. I hope she's not married. In fact, I know she's not. She must smell like candles and woman deodorant with a mix of body odor. The womanly odor always comes through and that's fantastic because it makes them part of the species.

"Hey, Elena II, would you have dinner with me?" I'd ask with a bouquet of flowers in my arms after having knocked on her front door. I'd be dressed in a tuxedo I found at a thrift store that I've wanted to purchase since last year. I'd have a small vehicle parked outside to take us to a Chinese restaurant. She'd smile, fasten her robe a little bit, but teasing me nonetheless. I've never had a girl flirt with me, actually. It must be because of the ligature scars. How do they know what actually happened? It could've been the serial killer, Al, who lived in the apartment above us for seven years. Elena II would say, "Of course. I'm glad you've been observing me. Our telepathy has been welcome company. It's like you've been inside me already, but not in a crude way. It's like our bodies and our minds are contoured in the perfect manner so that we fit together like puzzle pieces in the image of Europa." She'd open her robe just a bit, not nearly enough to expose the entirety of her brown nipples. We would get married at that point, but we wouldn't have a daughter because she would have to be named ELENA III and that's too much like calculus.

Again, tonight, I watch her and she's dancing this time in a sexy nightgown. I imagine she listens to music they play loudly in hip nightclubs. I can see her face so well—her high cheekbones, hair as straight as math, a nose so perfect it should be in a gallery, and a mouth as small and kissable and lovable as teddy bears. And then, as I'm lying in bed, I guess I fall into a deep slumber. I envision Elena II naked with her boobs swaying as we dance awkwardly facing each other. She mumbles something about "loving my neurons and the endearing, lovable people they create." Of course, my loins leak, and I'm half hoping to have a wet dream. "Come near me and never leave," I say with a prize-winning grin. She approaches me.

With her right hand, she unveils a third breast from a flesh pocket under her left boob. The third breast is less inflated and has no nipple, but something that looks like an anus. "I'll save you from suicide," Elena II exclaims. "It'll never have to be an option ever again." I reach out to her like an adolescent and grapple with the third breast. It terrifies me. "Don't be hesitant, D, I won't bite." So, I squeeze it gently and it doesn't feel like a human boob. There's sand inside it. "You've always needed a mother. An infant shouldn't come out of a corpse." I can't get over the curve of her hips. She grins like she's going to replace my galaxy.

And then she unfurls her umbilical cord from what I thought was a human belly button.

The cord is bruised as if it was a buried secret. She's still grinning like this event is nothing new in the world—just some sexual practice of the upper middle class. "Don't worry," she says, "We won't do bondage. We'll take it slow." Her fingers are long, spaghetti-like, and her nails are clipped short. I watch as she opens the end of her umbilical cord. It has the maw of an eel and I swear I see it mouth some silent words like "new womb," "no world." She beckons me with her index finger. "D, I want you deep inside me. I've never been this wide open for any other man or woman." She pries open the mouth of the cord as if it could exhort some dictator's cuss and come to life. "Would you put it in? Would you, please, just for me?" I don't know what to do and I don't want to do it. Elementary school and psychiatrists don't prepare you for experiences of this magnitude. I do begin to unzip my pants, but hesitate. I'm shaking like some queer. "There you go," she comments. "Don't you want my uterus? It's the source of all life. Crawl inside me for a lifetime or two." I take off my pants down to my white underwear. What real man wears white underwear anymore?

"What will happen... in *there*?" I ask. "What will it feel like?" I reach into my underwear as if I were actually going to unveil my pathetic appendage. I'm wholeheartedly mortified. It's a bit small, and the substandard doctors messed up my circumcision.

"If you inhabit my uterus, you'll create a new form of life that will never die, even after committing suicide." Her third breast jiggles from her heavy breathing. I've never seen someone so attractive and extraterrestrial.

"Should I wear a condom?"

She laughs because that truly is a ridiculous question. "No, silly, we're going to remake you inside me. You will never be sad again. You'll look exactly the same and your thoughts will be modifications on the old ones, but you'll be able to cope. You'll always be able to cope. Don't you want that for the rest of eternity?" I stare at the mouth of her bruised umbilical cord, offering itself to me, and my pathetic appendage is about to enact something unthinkable. "This is the NEW INTERCOURSE," she says.

I startle myself awake with my mouth agape, but I don't dare shriek. I sweat profusely and my bed linen is soaked. Oh God, there's semen smeared inside my underwear! A wet dream is something twelve year-old boys wish for, but not a middle-aged man. It's so pleasurable at first (some claim it's better than the real thing), but to me it's so absolutely tragic upon awakening. It's a liquid epidemiologists obsessively ruminate about as the source of melancholy, radical impulsivity, and mass murder. It saturates so deeply into all material and smells like detestable memories. My imaginary lovers affect me exponentially more than my family or my enemies.

I get out of the bed, my sheets dirtier than poverty, and walk over to the window. Elena II is still there, just standing with an erect posture and contemplating the monotony of existence. And then Elena II, turning toward me as I stand there in my white underwear, sees me staring at her and gasps with an expression of a baby seal that's about to be clubbed. She flips me off with a vigorous middle finger, screams something directly at me that I'll never hear, and lowers the blinds.

I am, largely, the common creepy monster. There's nothing special about me whatsoever.

And that's how Elena II and I get divorced. No alimony is demanded. I still care for her deeply, don't get me wrong, but it's better that I let her go. They say if you truly love someone, you may have to let them go. She did ignite the passion in me for an actual human woman. No foam latex wife for me. Maybe I did want to have a daughter named ELENA III, but Elena II no longer exists. My reality is shattered. Maybe the dream of being reborn with the ability to cope will still come true and I'll survive with the ability to endure my thoughts, the dust, all fucking women's glares of disgust, all the arrogant and muscular men, and my mother who hated me so much she forced herself to die while pushing me out through her hole.

Shit, Dad will be home soon and he'll look for me like he always does because he worries about me, so I'd better weep now. It's better to put a timeframe on weeping. It's only 6:36 in the evening. I have hours before I can go to sleep and anticipate the next day. I'd better get to it, then. I've wept so deeply into my yellowed, foul-smelling pillow thousands of mornings, afternoons, and nights. My life is bracketed by weeping. It's OK, though. I will perish after enduring middle-age and senility. Tear ducts of the insane go to the epicenter of Hell.

I get up this morning and there's a note from my dad on the fridge. "Coffee is ready. I went to the park early. Leave a note if you leave." I fold the note carefully and save it in an envelope in my drawer like I always do.

I have been saving his notes to me since childhood.

Maybe I should cut off my feet or scoop out my brains and plop them in the sink to spite him. Just think how the garbage disposal would eat that. It's the old lady, Lydia, I know it. That's cool. The old man needs a girl. I should be happy for him, but I hope he knows how to use condoms. I wonder if Lydia can still get pregnant. I've heard of a woman getting pregnant at sixty-eight. Well, I wouldn't want him to get any venereal disease. That's the last thing this family needs.

Mommies and Crimes

As far as my depression goes, it goes something like this. When I'm not depressed, I'm not depressed at all and being depressed sounds absolutely awful, the worst thing in the world, almost downright *immoral*. But when I start to get depressed, I feel like getting *more* depressed, so I lie in bed completely still in order to get immensely depressed. So, if I get a little depressed, I yearn for gigantic depression; so as I see it, me *being* depressed causes me to *want* to be depressed enormously; subsequently, *I get really fucking depressed* since I am, in fact, getting what I want. So, when I'm really, really, really depressed, I'm actually ecstatic! I'm enamored of my obese depression so badly I want to blow my head off! Of course, when I'm not depressed, I despise depression because, of course, I'm not depressed and, therefore, the concept of killing myself seems ludicrous! However, usually I'm utterly depressed and I've learned to savor my depression which, in itself, would make *anyone* want to kill themselves; but I actually *have* learned to *love* my suicide—love it so greatly, I'm totally addicted to suicide! And yet, when I'm not depressed (which is not often since I like *exactly* where I am in this miasma of shit and mulch and mangled grammar), I do believe in God, which proves *not* being depressed is *against* human nature since we know that God doesn't exist. This realization propels me toward *incurable* depression and exhilaration about the idea of being annihilated.

I don't bother to drink any coffee this morning.

Maybe it's time for me to find my own wife. I like a little chub to nibble on. As far as her personality goes? I just hope she's not into abstract painting or yoga. I hope she shaves her armpits. It'd be great if she were into philosophy. I've been delving into the literature. They're positing that the internet will come to life or some stupid thing like that. I've been reading about the ethics of cryogenics—you know where they freeze your head or whole body to resuscitate you in the future. I guess the ethical dilemma is that you would wake up, shocked, on a new version of Earth—no friends, no family, no home, no community, but simply an overwhelming sense of nostalgia. Communicating with humanoids would have morphed and evolved so radically. Certainly, email and video-cams would be for the primitives. The New Earth would have legislated against the use of mouths. But there's nothing like being terminally alive. I wonder if my girlfriend would want to be terminally alive with me, but always on the verge of suicide. We'll save the miracles for later.

Dad comes back from his outing and has the glow of infatuation. I'm not jealous, no really, I'm not. We watch television, but I don't pay attention. I daydream about what it would be like to roam the continents without being able to die, traipsing around the equator forever, enduring the sun, and coming across the same strangers maybe fifty years later after I've rounded the earth, except I would still be the current D you hear from now. Ah, it's a dumb idea and it makes me very anxious in the gut, so I'd better stop thinking about the possibilities of eternity just in case I project my terror into the atmosphere.

Dad turns to me. "Why don't you find a nice girl?" He smiles and takes off his fedora. I forgot he is balding. "You need a pretty girl to keep you company and take care of you a little bit."

"I've been thinking about that lately. I met this woman, but it didn't work out."

"You didn't tell me about that?"

I couldn't bear to tell him it was a marriage through my bedroom window, my telescope, and an inability to escape my inner world. Nothing is as real, or more embarrassing, than your failed daydreams.

Dad cradles the fedora in his lap. He's about to speak, but then I envision him in his coffin wide awake. His eyes would have changed to violet by then. That happens after eight months in the grave. Decomposition is as painful as being skinned, except lasts many, many years. Dad would get used to agony and suffocation, and he'd even begin to relish suffering. Suffering ignites adrenaline and euphoria, even upon the dead. That's why some insane persons cut their legs off at the knee. That's why Civil War amputees, with no anesthesia available or invented, shrieked in ecstasy as the gushing limb plopped onto the ground after the savage doctors hacked it off.

Dad turns to me with his fedora still in his lap. "Why don't you go back to church with me? There are plenty of nice girls there. Maybe even someone like you." He smiles, hope flushing back into his cheeks and eyes—the doting father desperately trying to cure the son.

"I'm not going out with the retard at church," I say. "Is that what you mean by someone like me?" I look into his eyes and recognize that I have disappointed him again. I look away at some woman in tight jeans on the television. "The retard is happier to be alone. She doesn't realize she is even alone. I, on the other hand, realize the unpleasantness of being without the opposite sex, but have not been able to properly develop the means, personal habits, and drive to devise a good, successful plan at procuring a girl. There may be half a dozen girls out of six billion who would be able to tolerate me. And would I even want them? Would they be fastidiously ugly and horrible and bitchy? Would they even be able to love me, or would it just be absolute silent tolerance? Men like me are a dime a dozen, but it was better when they warehoused us among nuclear waste and sluts of either gender."

My father stares at the television and shakes. I

know he is not far from crying. I have never seen him cry. Never. He must've emoted greatly when I popped out onto the slab and the love of his life, my mother Elena, lay there wide-eyed like heaven-bound meat. All the blood, the stiffness of my mother who was once a vibrant spirit, the silence in the hospital room as the doctors had no training to console men like my father, and me, the new baby, still connected to the afterbirth, shrieking and shrieking as I had begun to comprehend my life's predicament. My brute instinct and gumming for the teat would never come to fruition. I'm sure, then, my father cried and cried—for my mother, for himself, and maybe even for me. He has never talked about it and never will. "Just come to church with me," he beckons, still blankly staring at the television. "You need goodness, D, goodness, to surround you." He turns toward me, but looks at my chin. "You don't have to find a girl right away. Don't you want to be good, to be around good people?" He clasps the crucifix around his neck.

And I know he's probably right. I don't need to believe in God to go. What would it hurt? I used to go when I was younger. It wasn't so painful. I admit, it was rather boring and none of the scripture spoke to me, but I was around a community with purpose. Sure, maybe they were all deluded and a bunch of hypocrites, but for a couple of hours they had focus, equanimity of spirit, calmness, and maybe even a sense of love for their fellow man. What I don't tell Dad as he looks at my chin is that I spoke to God before my hanging and God was a Neanderthal. Sure, he was a world species and spoke every language that would ever be invented. He was kind. He did not say bad things or even encourage me to jump into the noose. It's just that his presence didn't calm me or make me feel even the slightest bit better. You see, I do believe that vision was real. That, indeed, was the Father of our universe. Even his compassionate rhetoric couldn't comfort that twelve year old boy. My infant head and shoulders, busting out of her opening, were too much for my mother. My very existence pained her to death.

I killed my mother.

God and heaven can't do the job effectively. Miracles are suited for certain people, and not others. The noose was, and is, my destiny. But I can't tell my father that while we're peripherally watching the bouncing, tight-jeaned women slink around the television for no good reason. I don't mean to be a bad son and constantly fail him. I mean, I should go to church. I should kneel before the Lord, not out of belief, but out of gratitude for my father. *My* dad. I turn away from his hopeful expression, look at the tight butts on the television, and exclaim, "I can't, Dad. No, I won't. It's not even about the retard girl, Dad."

He puts his fedora back on and reaches for the remote control. His hands look more and more decrepit. He changes the channel to a new talk show. It's hosted by this woman they imported from below the border—a brown girl with blonde hair, big-busted, curvy and full of verve. He used to watch her in his language, but prefers the English version now. The show is called *Elena!* As he becomes absorbed by the talk show host, Elena, his interest in me wanes. It has to be that way for him. There's only so much a father can take.

"I just can't do it," I mutter, ashamed. I reach up to my throat with my right hand and caress the scars of that noose-rodeo from adolescence. Actually, and this may seem crazy, but I was *totally successful.* My father doesn't consciously know it, of course, but I can see it in his eyes that he grieves for the loss of his entire family. The Middle-Eastern manager at the corner store where I buy groceries doesn't know I was successful at suicide. But I'm convinced that I was. I was absolutely successful. I committed suicide.

I notice my father stealing glances at me from

the other side of the sofa while watching the television. Don't you see, I'm in a quagmire of zombie mulch? Dad, I eat eyeballs for lunch. Then, I turn my fuzzy attention to the talk show on the television: *Elena!* She's an attractive brown woman in her later thirties, throwing her hips every which way as she declares empathy for her guests—always the grungiest of humanoids. This episode, they mostly have hillbilly children with their culpable parents seated on stage. Elena is not used to interacting with the hillbillies. It's not that they're bad. They just have their own vernacular, a peculiar thought process, and lives consumed by solitude and fear and rage.

"Today," Elena exclaims with the microphone a bit too close to her mouth. "We are visiting with a tragic, but lucky group of children. These poor boys and girls, leading sad lives throughout the most and all of the day..." Elena hasn't been in the country long enough to quite perfect the language. None of us, no citizen worth mentioning, knows any of the grammar anyway. But the casual verbiage, if mangled, can extract giggles from the masses. She mangles a sentence badly. But it makes her endearing. Plus, since all men and lesbians have begun watching her on TV as well, she exudes lust out of every pore—even through the television. "These children, for one reason onto others, attempted the desperate act of suicide." She sweeps her arm across the stage, pointing to each of the meager-looking kids—mostly girls, but one obese boy—as each of them just stares at the carpet, not wanting to be on stage at all. Whose idea was it to bring these barely living children onto national television? Did the producers of the show pay them handsomely, or their vile parents? Did the children at least get trust funds? Will they live to inherit anything?

Dad and I watch as the children hesitate to answer Elena's awkwardly probing questions, delivered, of course, with a quiet voice and through lipstick so red every adolescent boy would want to smooch her. Most of the surviving children sit rock-still and answer the questions dutifully, not elaborating on the gory details of why they wanted to take a nosedive into the abyss. It actually makes for bad television. But Elena is persistent. She is a like a prosecutor, but with a womanly demeanor, always saying she is sorry, etc. The obese boy who, if you look closely enough, has an upside-down cross tattooed on his fatty forehead. But he weeps in frenzy. He weeps because his life depends on it, at least in that moment—until he returns to school the next day, not as an object of empathy, but as a fat fucking boy who stupidly and sinfully tried to kill himself. And even worse, he wept like a pussy on national television! To be suicidal and famous—it's the hope of every mental patient with the guts to admit it.

And then the scrawniest girl with a once tattered dress, but was recklessly sewed back to a garb suitable for the criminally insane. She stands up waving her index finger first at Elena, then at the audience, and finally at her gargantuan, diabetic mother. The girl wants to expel the raging succubus from inside her gut, but she can't. She holds a device to her throat that enables her to speak properly. You know those devices for the speechless that sound like 1950s robots? "Mother... and... all of... you people." She lowers the device and wipes her eyes. "I came... here... to tell my... story and... why I did what... I did." She is visibly trying to hold back tears, knowing how the fat boy's tears would drive him to a successful attempt on his life in no later than two years from now. "But... it's really none... of your businesses... we're on the welfare... we eat cereal for dinner... a lot of sugar... and my dad is on the disability while... Mom... turns tricks..."

"Honey!" her gargantuan mother raises her fist, but realizes beating her daughter on national television would brand her as the hillbilly that she is. "That's simply not true! I'm a massage therapist!" She covers her mouth and her fingers are so fat, they are basically melded together like humanoid flippers.

The audience gasps and laughs and whoops. Yes, finally, it all comes out! What an afternoon! What a show!

The little girl with the robot's tenor continues. "No... my mom turns tricks... it's all we have for the canned ravioli and... sugar-coated corn flakes and... corn chips. Do you... know... Mom?" The girl can barely keep back the tide of emotion. Her head is a bit big for the slim body of hers, but maybe this display will give her the courage to move forward and escape the hillbilly biosphere. Either that or her mom will decapitate her when they get back home—after getting the check from the television show, of course. "Mom's regular trick..." she turns to Elena. "He's... thin and grins every other... tooth." The girl turns toward the audience. "This man—he calls himself Elias, but he's... had many names throughout... history. He's liked me too... much... up me..." She stops then as her fat-ass mom stands up, swaying this way and that way, but there's no direction to run but up, baby. "Mom... got more for... that. I stabbed... my throat... seven times... so they couldn't... put anything in... it... no more." The girl puts the voice-box in her pocket and simply walks off the stage. The audience is silent. Elena sits on the edge of the stage, holding the microphone like the flaccid nightmare between men's thighs. Children's services would be called. Elena would be interrogated by the producers and she would make a public apology. The little girl with the robot voice would feel pride and rage for many years to come as she moves in with a new, prosperous family. The nation would demand that she have the best things in life. They would try to prepare her for an education, proper etiquette, the ambition of the upper middleclass, the brainpower of women in this current decade... but little do they know that she is destined to repeat this day of triumph in her mind for the rest of her life. The experience would consume her and she would never want to leave her bedroom. You see, she had wanted to take the knife with a venomous, striking blow to Elias and her gargantuan mother's throats. The girl would smile with breast-thumping pride; ruminate at age thirty-six in the psychiatric hospital womb of the impoverished she calls home; choke on the memories of protuberances in her scarred, puny throat; and thrive in her immaculate hospital gown for decades after our nation and her new family give up on her.

Dad, too, will give up on me. He won't forget my hardboiled face, or the stubborn frown or the odor, the socks, the weeping, or even the dried droplets of urine on the rim of the toilet. I wipe my face with my right palm. Jesus, that didn't help, my palm is sweaty, too. It's not that I'm crying or want to cry; it's just that I stink. I smell my armpits and notice that Dad is staring at the matted carpet, the television off now, the living room quiet. All anyone can hear is my snorting. I keep doing it and doing it. It's not the snot, but the utter lack of anything to declare. *Dad, I'm the living dead!* I could scream. He wouldn't believe me, anyway. He would continue to lock his vision onto the carpet. *What is it? Are there ghosts intertwined with the pennies and pubic hair?* I want to ask him. My head is a yam. Shit, I *am* deformed. Stop it. I clench my fist and raise it right in front of my eyes. My heart is a clenched, seven-fingered fist that pumps out a season's worth of blood and shame into my middle-aged body. I'm only in my fucking mid-thirties.

"Who was the girl? What was her name?" Dad turns toward me and I know he's been thinking about her ever since I said I "met" one of those females. He takes a wrinkled handkerchief to his forehead. What worrying lies behind that forehead?! It's all he wants for me and for himself—a girl with any name, a generic body, a disembodied voice, plain-clothed, any race whatsoever. He reaches into the inner pocket of his blazer. He pulls out a big, silver coin—definitely from another country. He palms it and reaches out toward me as if to give me this alien currency. What would a humanoid buy with alien dollars? I mean, what the hell is he thinking? His palm is right next me—an offering of sorts. I'm confused. The coin must mean something to him, so I take it from him and slip it into my pajama pocket. "Give it to that girl or another girl when you marry one. I know you will."

I lower my head because I can't stand the hotness of his parental eyes. So, I shake my head. I hear something jiggle inside my head. Shit, I think that was a loose neuron. "What am I supposed to do with it?" I ask.

"With the silver coin?" he asks.

I can't imagine how he's interpreting my question. I blush. The buttons are snapped over my groin. "Yeah, Dad, with the coin."

He slouches. Fuck, he *is* defeated. He never would've made it as a professional football coach. They never slouch. They have titanium balls. Women want nothing to do with balls like those because they're terrifying. Only God does.

"It was your Mom's," Dad replies with his stinky exhale. Maybe he sees the end coming—my wedding or my funeral.

I palm the coin inside my pajama pocket. It's cold, but not like ice. Am I supposed to carry this thing around with me now? Is that what children do with items of the dead? I wonder what Mom would have bought with it had she put up a better fight during that last *push*. Or maybe the coin was an emblem of something important: her first meager payment from her job at the sweatshop, or perhaps a dumb "gift from Santa" left under her pillow. Foreigners are always mixing up the Tooth Fairy and Santa Claus anyway.

But my mom's fingerprints are on this coin some-where—the last trace of her. Well, that should touch my heart! I'm about to give my dad a big, mushy hug.

Again, he simply stares at the carpet, and shivers—a drenched, drenched man.

Did his old lady dump him already? I'll stomp the shit out of her plutonium head.

I'd better *not* hug him. I'd better *not* let him down. I'd better not say *anything* at all.

Marriage and the Confidence Loop

The pressure's on. But I'm really fucking prepared this time. I wake up. It's 11:42 AM. Almost noon and the time of the gods, so I stretch and do calisthenics in my mind, jog in place a little bit, think of shaving, get out some underwear to take a shower, but I just change out of my dirty underwear into clean ones and fling the dirty ones under the bed.

Under the bed.

There are heads under there.

I open the closet and I actually have a lot of clothes for a man on disability. Most importantly, I have acquired two suits: the beige, linen suit with a matching spotty, brown tie, stringy belt, kerchief and toad lapel-pin for wooing the ladies and eventually getting married; and the black, freshly pressed suit with form-fitting dress shirt, suspenders you actually have to button under the waistband of your pants, a special pair of polyester black socks, a red velvet bowtie and a fake rose for my lapel.

Of course, the black suit is the one I'll die in.

Today, I'll find my wife. She's out there in the wilderness of the city, the street fucks, Goths, dead letters and old stamps, torsos sleeping in nursing homes, the sleeping train operator who can't get off the glue, and the prostitutes who are trying to make just enough money to make it to Miami. Aida! Shit, I forgot about her. How can that even be possible? She's the only woman who has spooned me, although I do have to give her money. I've never developed a sincere bond with her, though. She *is* quite the number and she even let me smell her breasts once. I think she was drunk that time. I don't believe it has anything to do with giving her money. I just don't think we have anything in common, although she *is* a wonderful human being inside—so thoughtful to help someone like me.

Like I said, I want someone who is into philosophy, or anatomical drawings, or robotics, or able to disprove gravity in some way no scientist has ever thought of. I tried to disprove gravity once—and may have come close—but it could've been a delusion caused by the neuron that leaked out of the socket of my missing tooth. I want a smart girl. I think I'm good enough. Dad says I have a nice frame, whatever that means. I don't think women are into frames, though. A woman likes a man who is good at math, can recite poetry but has a smirk on his face conveying *this really is pussy shit*, probably has a tight bottom, is an expert in bed and wherever it is they *engage*, will kiss them good night and mean it, and will try really, really hard to like her parents. I have heard of the career component, too. Yeah, I don't have that going for me yet. I have the rest of the checklist down, though. Pretty much, anyway. I think the beige, linen suit with the accoutrement puts a special touch and highlights the preciousness of my spirit.

So, first I'll pick up a bouquet of roses, even though I don't have a girl yet, but I'll have a potential wife by the end of the evening, so I should be prepared with the pleasantry of roses. Roses are a nice gesture from a gentleman. It will depend on how much the roses cost, though. There are always carnations, or maybe I'll just buy one rose. Shit! There's so much to juggle, to weave and maneuver through (especially all the filthy and clean clothes intertwined on my bedroom floor like an orgy of skins), a man can get really, really overwhelmed. I mean, I'm sweating out succubae from my pores and it's already past lunch time! I don't have time to eat now. I'll down one of my dad's chocolate nutritional drinks, maybe two, and that'll keep me going until I get married or at least engaged. Shit! I forgot the ring! I'll pick one up somewhere. The prickly, Southern dude at the thrift store will give me a deal on one of his finer pieces of jewelry in the box under the cash register. I hope my wife is pretty. In fact, I've made up my mind! I'm absolutely confident that she is! What was I thinking? I'm going to go for it, fuckos. That means I *really do* have to shower and use shampoo and soap on all the body parts, not just the ones you're accustomed to touching. God, the body is so revolting, so despised, and so *filthy*—especially certain areas and convergences of flesh that house vile, vile material. No wonder I don't shower as much as my dad demands, but who wants to grapple with a handful of clumped-together creepiness that your body produces on all its own, without you being part of any decision-making process? I mean, *really*, morning after morning of grappling with vile, bodily coalescences? Would you shake that hand after a grooming like that? Some ordinary humanoids would say the opposite conclusion should be reached: take a shower several times per week, at least. But I have a peculiar rhetorical process. Sometimes, I out-argue myself and that's when Dad knocks on the bedroom door to tell me stop debating myself in a variety of high and bellowing voices. OK! The shower! The suit! The flowers! And I'm out that fucking front door.

It's 5:03 PM. I've got it all by the balls: I have the suit on with the tie, near-leather belt, lapel-pin, etc., and my hair is perfectly parted with pomade I stole from the drugstore (I *had* to buy the ring and the flowers). Actually, after all that showering and running around, I feel pretty goddamn confident—even though (and this is a big *even though*) my bitchy ancient neighbor (I believe her name is actually *Justin*) bellowed at me from the bowels of her chain-smoking existence: "I haven't seen your crazy ass since they lowered you down from that noose!" And she giggled with the cigarette dangling from her pinched, fleshy hole. Ha, ha, ha!

That threw me for a *terrible* confidence loop, but I would recover quite well, thank you, ladies and gentlemen. And it's not even true, what the old broad fucking screamed at me! I *have* seen her since being lowered limply from my precious noose at age twelve! "Don't you remember?" I nearly bellowed back at her, "When I stalked you for seventeen days straight with a cleaver in my backpack, fresh and pink ligature marks around my throat, and I wielded the meat-obliterating-machine in my right fist when no one else was around, and to your horror as you dared to glance at me running toward you, I'd be hacking at the image of your burlap head barely down the way from me, but you couldn't totally be sure it was me because I wore pantyhose over my head to disguise my repulsive, nearly-dead, twelve-year-old self! Don't you remember that, you old, deep-fried corpse? And, you know what? Those were *your* nunnery pantyhose that I stole from your dresser while you snored and moaned and hankered for a lumberjack; but don't get me wrong, I bleached the shit out of those pantyhose before I donned them and terrorized you until this moment in your old-ass life when the vision of me as a grown man triggered you out of senility to force out a rather tasteless insult about a young boy in a noose!" But like I said, I simply passed by her and focused on the godly lit pathway to my future wife, or at least girlfriend. I blocked the shrieking, female corpse *out*! And I didn't need her pantyhose over my shamed face. Dad was absolutely correct. Getting a girl is the best thing in the whole wide world, etc. What a man he is... what a goddamn man ...

I arrive at her condominium and my pants are riding up my butt. I have to put the flowers on the ground (sorry, soon-to-be wife) to pull the pants out from my butt. Before picking up the flowers, I look at my hands—meaty, bloated and veined just like Mommy's after she was embalmed. What a horrible thing to taste, I mean to think, God, I keep messing up languages in my head. I didn't mean to refer to you like that, Mom. Your hands were beautiful going six feet down into the still sea of dirt and *phalluses*. Damn, again! I mean *worms*! So, I pick up the flowers. Why am I so fucking old and without children? Without a wife that is glad to see me even if my middle age is suddenly upon me? Without a sports car that zips in and out of traffic and I'd go so fast, so fast through life I wouldn't care about the people I hit. I wouldn't care about anything except the lovely life I have at home.

I hide behind a large bush. Do you think the linen suit is good enough? I could be the meanest man at the disco. Do they make discos anymore?

I've been waiting for a few hours. God, I thought I had her schedule down. I turn to face the traffic and see that an elderly couple stringing along a phlegm-sized dog are staring at me. The old wife, the doting wife, holds the old man's hand as if she were tethered to him to keep her from floating into outer space toward one of Jupiter's loneliest moons. I guess I look like a serial killer just crouching here behind a bush and waiting. What kind of serial killer wears a linen suit and brings flowers to his victims? I turn away from them, pretending to be that ideal husband zipping through life and not caring about anything but family, hamburgers, television with the bodacious babes, and my wife. Oh, here she comes from out of the condominium.

I creep out from behind the bush and fix my grin and snag the pants away from the groin. Groining is for another time.

She sees me as I bear the flowers in front of my body and with a tenuous grin, standing at attention because I'm a good boy—no serial killer here.

She's with a rather large mustachioed man. He may be Hells Angel. He may be one of the bouncers in front of the entrance to Purgatory. He does sweat, and looks on fire, in the overgrown, fake fur coat.

I stream up to her, not minding the gargantuan

man. "I brought you flowers," I say, confronting Elena II with my wholehearted grin; no tomorrows, I say all the time, there are none, especially for this nincompoop. I'm shifting and shifting my weight and I remember I forgot to change my underwear.

At first, she smiles as if she remembers our marriage; so vast, the only means of communication was telepathy and the like. And her umbilical cord...

"Who *are* you?" she asks with her spindly hands on her hips. It's the fashionable jeans and the sashay that endear my heart even more.

Her Godzilla with the fur coat steps in front of her. She peeks from behind the mass. I, somehow, didn't put two-and-two together. "You know this guy, Jess?" he asks. His arms are crossed and he has a manhandled expression as if he could shatter gods with his teeth.

"Elena II, it's me. Has it really been that long? I think not."

Elena II starts weeping and weeping as if the AIDS-infected baboons had finally come out from under her bed to eat her. She drops to the ground and the doorman strides out. He has a manhandled expression as well. He's not so big, though.

Godzilla gets right up into me, but I only make it to his chest. "What did I do?" I ask. "Please, tell me," I say in the undertow of my voice. I'm sucking in air while I speak, instead of propelling my voice outward. I can't see much of Elena II, except her flailing arms which have begun to bleed. Even from here, I can see the blood...

"I'm so sorry..." I whimper.

"How did you know her daughter's name, Elena? Huh, motherfucker?!" He pushes me down to the ground and my ass bone nearly shatters. I don't mind pain. In fact, I welcome it with a hug. Pain, great friend! "Are you the one who kidnapped Elena, you fucking pervert? You take Elena away from her mother?" Godzilla puts his steel-toe boot on my groin; not this kind of groining do I wish for, nor deserve.

"There's a misunderstanding," I reason. "I must've thought she was someone else..."

"Where's Elena, you fucking molesting faggot?!" He takes his steel-toe boot away from my groin and, at first I think he's come back to the Enlightenment. "Stand up, creepo."

I get up and it seems I soiled myself. I'm hoping the shit won't show through the beige, linen suit. I have on my ruined marriage suit. *Elena II*, I think, *I'm sorry, but I'll come back when you return to your name. You really have a daughter named ELENA III? The umbilical sexing really consummated us? It's ungodly, insane impregnations!*

Godzilla wrecks my face with his right fist. It's as big as my head. I would've guessed he is left-handed. I begin to let go, slowly, some tears, but it's like I finally need a mommy, because I don't, mankind to whom I shriek, I don't, because Mommy abandoned me before my first breath.

The doorman breaks it up. "Henry, Henry, shit, you're gonna get the cops called on you." Godzilla backs off and lifts Elena II to her wobbly feet. "I think that's the fucko who kidnapped Elena, Jess' daughter."

"Shit, man," the doorman coughs up. "Fuck. Better call the cops. Fuck, man, fuck, fuck."

Godzilla, "Yeah, triple-fucked in the ass, is what it is..."

As they both exchange "Oh my Gods," I bolt up and sprint like the badass Olympian I never knew I was. Shit, I dropped the flowers! Elena II can have them once she realizes who I am, who I was, and we had ELENA III. I didn't kidnap her! Why would I kidnap my own flesh-and-blood? Godzilla begins to chase after me, but his heft prevents any kind of real pursuit and, if ever I felt alive, it is absolutely now. *Now* is it, babies. "You child-molesting fuck, you're leaking diarrhea all over the fucking sidewalk!" My butt bone electrocutes me, so much pain, and my face throbs to hell and must look more like an organ that belongs inside me, under my ribs, never to be seen by its human owner. *Now* is a short time. There are very few nows left in existence. Television has prevented that. The internet, sleeping in the afternoon, looking at yourself in the mirror—naked and fat and alone: they all deafen the nows. And then, I'm at my front door and I realize I smell like a plump babe who's sprayed feces all over the walls. God-awful, I am. I haven't littered myself like this since maybe fourteen. So, not wanting Dad to discover me with my bowels inside-out, I open the front door slowly and see him on the couch. He's asleep with his fedora over his face. He slouches as if he's defeated. Even in sleep, you feel the burden of living up to the expectations you inherit from parental beatings. I walk past him, pat his shoulder, and direct myself to my room. I think of flopping onto my bare mattress fully-dressed and painted with my own manure. It would be a magnanimous sleep, so alive with pain, suffering, and shit. Jesus, even I can't do that. I've drawn a limit for maybe the second time in my life: I will shower. I take off my suit, careful not to get the floor too mucked up, and tie up my only marriage garb in a plastic garbage bag. My dad buys garbage bags for me, but I throw nothing away, except I guess, my future. I get naked—this I *do* like. Nude is fun. Bubble baths are fun! It's too late for a bubble bath, so I turn the water on full blast and test it to see how hot I can take it. I discover the hottest I can take, and turn it up a little more. I must push the envelope for once. And with reckless abandon, I leap into the lava and hold my shriek in my gut. Vomit starts to bubble up from my insides. But I'm showering away the shit and the muck. The tub is already brimming with a slew of browns, greens and yellows. I've made a responsible decision. I decide to get clean.

Her Repressed Angelic Feet

The marriage suit is forever defiled and now simply dead. I will never own another beige, linen suit quite like that one, nor will I ever own any marriage suit whatsoever.

There will be no marriage. Even if I bring my fist down hard on the desk, it won't change the past, present, or future. I'm genetically engineered. They switched a string of DNA when they invented me. No marriage for him, they said. No marriage, no woman, no soul. And the self-pity makes me even feel worse! I can't help it, I guess. Sperm has backed-up into my cerebellum. The protuberance in my underwear was engineered from steel fiber. No respectable woman wishes to rub up against steel.

There in the duct-taped box in the lower left corner of my closet is my infant death suit. Dad had it tailored for me to wear to Mom's funeral. I've looked at it once when my dad believed I should take it as my own property. I glanced at the crotch of it, how the baby must've been terrified all laced up for Mommy's burial. The infant dressed in black velvet (how fucking weird) as if the fat priest would throw it in with Mommy. Of course, I remember nothing. I do remember breast feeding from Mom's teat, but it must be a memory-implant or a psychiatric surgeon's April fool's joke on my maimed brain. So much goddamn breast milk...

I put on my grown-man funeral suit. It's one of the finest they had at the thrift store. It doesn't even smell bad—simply like the insides of soldiers before they die. Yes, even though marriage is probably off the table for me, I'm going out in search of a wife nonetheless. Not the Neanderthal women, the daughters of our primitive God. I can't stand a protruding forehead. I'm not down for the sagging boobs, or the overgrown pubes, nor the shaved ones I've seen in porn oh so many ages ago. Today, Dad left for the park and his old lady (if she exists) and didn't make coffee. He figures, in my middle age there's a time to make and imbibe my own caffeine. Responsibility is a terrible thing. Today I'll go without. But I grab his note on the fridge without reading it, fold it into a square, and place it in the envelope in my dresser with all the other notes from him.

I will go to funerals in search of the perfectly depressed and handsome woman.

Walking the half-mile of "funeral parlor row" (like the theater district I heard of in the Big Apple) where all the wakes and séances commence, and adjourn, I'm carrying a bulky bouquet of flowers. I had to use most of my savings for this lovely bouquet. The store owner—masculine, fat, stained t-shirt and mangled teeth—said in a high-pitched voice, "I can have it delivered. You don't have to carry it there." I put on my sun glasses before picking up the flowers. "You see," I said. "I have no idea where I'm going."

This is the last sojourn—my last travel on Earth (or at least in my freaky little town). OK, I'm a bit melodramatic. That's what they say on all the documentaries about our troubled family. "What's wrong with that boy D, he's so big-bellied and melodramatic? And he has the gumption to make his father clean up after him. Does his father clean his butt, too? Isn't the father an immigrant?" I tell those filmmakers that they are supposed to be unbiased. What's so special about our family, anyway? Are we werewolves or beheaded postal carriers? It's a great nation. Oh, yeah, the bouquet is getting friggin' heavy, but I'm almost at the first funeral parlor. Great! There are crowds there. It must be somebody famous, so I may meet a gorgeous superstar, or at least her aunt.

That's when I trip and fall face first onto the bouquet. Fuck! "Ha, ha!" some toothless murderer screams while driving past me in his white-trash pick-up truck. I ripped my pants a little bit. My knee is scraped, but face is OK. Well, it was never OK, but it's not bloody is what I mean. You can't go to a funeral of famous people wearing a blood-soaked face. I wipe my suit and hope no one will notice the rip in my suit pants. Go to hell, anyway! I deserve love!

I walk in and sit toward the back. Nobody says a thing. They're all consumed with themselves and consoling the elders of the crew. I don't see any famous people yet, so this must be the extended family. They have the VIPs in a separate wake behind the wall with a secret entrance. The open casket here has a fake body, but in the VIP room they have the real body to mourn. People with money and fame always get first dibs on mourning.

And then I notice there's another very small casket next to the big one. The small one is closed. No seeing him, right? It must be a baby. Does the big casket house the body of the little one's mother? How odd and tragic. I get wobbly kneed, yearning for malt liquor for the first time in about three years, and just stare straight ahead. Open big casket—closed tiny one. Are there real bodies in there? Are there really VIPs in another world with the real bodies sending them into outer space? One can never know these things for sure, so I just assume these, here, are the real, dead deal.

I step up to the big casket as if to say a prayer goodbye. At peace, the dead woman looks familiar and docile and approachable. Most women are not. Her black hair is thick as chocolate malt, and her head is heavy (I imagine) like a comforter filled with stones. She's definitely a woman from another country, judging from her olive skin and three birth marks on her face. Whites never have dark birthmarks. Maybe I went to school with her?

I'm about to cry. Some old women around me are touched and raise kerchiefs to their eyes. No, I didn't know this dead woman except in nostalgia; I never touched the intimacy hidden under those lacy panties. I've had none of that, but I weep. The dead make their loved ones alive, so alive because the dead are exhilarating, unlike most of life. I turn toward the small casket and nearly weep some more. An old woman with a shawl over her head brings me a kerchief as if she can see I *will* lose myself, fall to my bruised knees and pelt my head against the titanium casket of this babe. I won't be able to see him, or his name tattooed on his forehead. I hear people from that part of the world do that to dead children so God will recognize them in heaven. The dead baby could be Hobart, or Ignacio and Chimpy, but it could've been me in there if they hadn't cut me out or forced me through my mother's wretched vaginal opening. Whatever it was, and by whatever means, I barely made it out of my mother alive. *And thank God!* everyone exclaimed about me, the miracle baby. My father wept and laughed during alternate breaths. I wonder if my father was wearing his fedora when I plopped out and his wife closed her eyes for the last time.

I walk out and away of the funeral parlor. I will never see the dead mother and child again. They mean so much to me. Maybe they are my wife and child from another universe. Right now, the husband is about to commit suicide because it was he who put the gun to her head and forced her and their child to swallow the cyanide. In that way, he and I are satanically connected—an invisible spider web as strong as God's threads tethers us between universes. I am him, and he is me. We have different names. Each of us, now, has no wife or child. I'm on disability and he steals cars. But, whatever the minutiae of our small lives, our fathers feel sorry for us. This "feeling sorry" is one of the great mysteries of modern times. Our fathers wear fedora's to protect their heads from our satanic desires.

They love each of their sons for no good reason. They shouldn't. The *sons* should commit suicide in public, to a cheering and tumultuous crowd doing the tango. We're two halves of one person in parallel universes, tenuously connected by a clothesline.

As I cross the street wiping the tears from my eyes, a woman screams from behind me, "Hey, D, wait! I saw you in the funeral parlor! You were looking for me, right? You're looking for a wife in funeral parlors!" I rush across the street—not wanting to be side-swiped by a black man's sedan—still wiping my globes, pulling up loose pants, scraping the gum off the sole of dress shoe—all at the same time. In another era, I would be Charlie Chaplin. People would swarm to love and fondle me. "D, wait up," the woman hollers. I don't turn around (at least not quite yet). I don't recognize that throaty voice. Is she a smoker?

But, now, I do face her. I look into her hazel eyes as I have never looked into any woman's eyes. Is there something familiar there? Does my stomach reel from nostalgia? My groin sleeps and my heart even slows. "Who are you?" I ask. "How do you know my name?" I make sure my zipper is up and, thank God, it is. I hate it when you're talking to a bosomy redhead and she can't keep her glare off your groin. You take this as a sign of deep interest, but for some reason (perhaps it's the growing chuckle she expresses) you know this never could be true. She sees your yellowed briefs. I'm a bereft man-child who yearns for a teat, a pillow, perfume, and this woman not laughing at me. That's what has hurt so many, many times.

But this woman's eyes are affixed on my dying eyes. She sees that I am jaundiced. I *am* diseased. "Don't worry," I should say out loud to this sweet, brunette thing, "you can't catch it unless you stepped into my MRI." I redden since I'm now vocalizing my thoughts. Grown men who vocalize their thoughts are on the road to a hell reserved for hyenas and other flesh-eaters.

"Catch what, D?" she asks as she puts her tiny hand on my arm. Is this woman totally out of her fucking mind? Does she know what I am? I lived in the apartment below a serial killer for seven years, eating his lusts by osmosis, now collecting the disability check because I *do* have the disease. "I *do* have the disease," I exclaim. She takes her hand away from my arm, wipes it on her jeans and smiles as if angels were tickling her. "You don't have a disease, D, plus I don't know who you're having a conversation with. It's probably not me. But I always liked you nonetheless."

She's wearing tattered, leather sandals. Her feet! I remember and love those feet!

"You don't remember me, do you, D?" She wipes her palms on her jeans and reaches out her right hand. I shake it and her palm is a bit clammy. "I've waited for you all these years and I knew you'd come back," she says.

"Come back from where?" I'm about to pick my nose, but I know this would be unbecoming. "I never go anywhere." But I smile. This woman is paying attention to me and knows my name. No matter, though, because she probably has me mixed up for a thug.

"Or," she says, "maybe you came back from *when*."

Evolutions Are Mutations

The woman's name is Ellen and I've been waiting for this moment my whole life. After meeting each other, we've spent weeks slopping around the mattress, but always with our clothes on. It's OK. It's the happiest I've ever been. I'm sorry I haven't been more in touch. I know she's using me for something, but no matter. The light in her room is less dank than mine. Plus, she smells like some illuminated animal; a good animal, not a flesh-eater. Today, I can tell by the way she's cupping my moist groin that this will be the day of reckoning—good or bad, it doesn't matter. There is no time for details, how the love sojourn came to this point. It's just the simple, adolescent crush delayed for thirty-five years.

We fall back into her down pillows. They might as well be clouds. "You know how I know you?" Ellen asks.

"Of course I don't. I've asked you a million times." I turn toward her as if she was my true wife and we've been doing this year after year.

"You're father's a great man," she says. "He's a bit stuck in his ways, but I'm sorry we hurt him the way we did." She picks her teeth with a ballpoint pen she found on the nightstand.

My face crumbles. "You know him?"

"Come on, D, you've appeared in my world again to finish an act we started years ago. I'm sorry you and I, especially me, hurt all these people for so many years." She turns toward me and strums my thinning hair with her index finger. "Think, D, think."

"I just remember your feet. They're like faces at the ends of your legs, like they're gonna suffocate in those shoes."

I can see from this vantage point that her ceiling is about to cave in. It's stained with water and sewage. Always, the sewage. It gets you every time. "When you were twelve and I was ten, we fucked," she says in between exhales, now suddenly smoking a cigarette. "We fucked meaningfully and I'd never have it like that again. We were babies. Why did we do that thing we shouldn't have known how to do? We did it anyway and we loved each other, so much we made a suicide pact, a pact that our sexing would be our last, best thing on Earth. You had to go and get your own noose, didn't you, D?"

I scoot away from her and sit on the edge of her bed. If leaping off the edge of the bed would land me in a deep, deep sea, I would leap. But it's just a couple of inches to the floor. "How do you know about that?" I ask, not wanting to face her, thinking maybe I would be facing Mom.

"I was there, D, because we were young and made the SUICIDE PACT. We were babies and we hated it all. You hung yourself and I chickened out. I went to your funeral and committed suicide three weeks later."

I get up in her face, baring my canine teeth, about ready to savage her expression. "I AM NOT DEAD!"

"Yeah, that's the problem, D," she exclaims as she pushes my lightweight threats away with her hand. "We both successfully committed suicide, but we didn't die. Our parents buried us, but now they've forgotten. It's like nothing has happened. Or, at least they pretend like nothing happened." She drags on the cigarette so delicately. She could've lived in the 1920s. "You and I, we both have the ETERNITY GENE. My daddy diagnosed me once. He's a psychiatric surgeon, the best in his field, and he recognized my suicide/living contradiction. We both have been on a trajectory to despise life, but when we end it, we come out the other end still alive. It's not like we died in our bodies, but the universe drops clone corpses into our parents' worlds to bury. But then again, the parents forget they bury the clone corpses, their children, and the bodies keep piling up, grave after grave, with the same names and headstones. We have the ETERNITY GENE and the SUICIDE GENE intertwined."

"How did your daddy... diagnose you?"

"He's a psychiatric surgeon. The ETERNITY GENE creates barely noticeable nodes along the genitals. He recognized them with his own, prying eyes."

I look at her groin and wonder what's there. These weeks, I thought there would be pleasure there. Now, I realize it's simply wet history strangling a ten-year-old girl's vagina, except now it belongs to a grown woman who's dead and alive with a penchant for suicide and climbing out of graves. Do I want what's down there? Of course I do! Who am I fucking kidding?! I've never seen a woman's vagina! But I suspect hers is terribly complicated.

"Are my ETERNITY AND SUICIDE GENES coupled around my genitals?" I ask and swallow, not knowing what's going down my throat.

"He has devised a cure, D. We will PROCREATE."

I pause and think of what the father and psychiatric surgeon has done to his daughter. Has he diagnosed her or simply turned her life upside-down? "Where is your father?" I ask.

"He lives in an eight-by-ten cube downstairs. I haven't seen him in about twenty years, now. Not too long after you died."

"Stop saying that!" and I begin to shake, to fever, and stomach turns to quills—so much down and feathers in my head, I might tickle myself to death.

"It was then that father did THE IMPLANT, but we *do* communicate through the pipes and play chess this way. I've waited for the right man to use THE IMPLANT. I waited for you to come back to me, D."

I realize the chair next to her perfectly-made bed is upholstered in deerskin. Don't ask me how I can differentiate meats and skins. It comes with the body;

it comes with the mind.

"You'd better sit," she says and sways in a way that I can see a millimeter of her right nipple—she reaching down to untie my shoes. She smells like down comforters and the most restful sleep. She's the best thing that has happened to me in this adult life, except maybe Dad. She says she knows me, but I don't know her. I have seen her feet before; perhaps on a mannequin in an expensive boutique store. This doesn't seem right. I don't normally fall in love with dolls.

"You really don't remember me, D?" She stands and wipes a bead of sweat from my cheek and she frowns the way mommies frown. "You're crying, D."

"Oh no, that's not crying. Sometimes my cheeks sweat, sometimes bleed; no, wait, take that back, not blood, just the insides coming out; like a leak of soul or whatever." The beads stream down my face now.

"Your insides are called 'crying.' Haven't you ever cried in front of a woman before?" She caresses my head, leaning into me, her bosom practically in my face, my groin enlivened like it never has been before.

The sun breaks the drapes and shows me light.

"It's OK. I know I was supposed to go with you that night when you wore the noose. I'm so sorry, D, I chickened out. You do know that I killed myself two days later, but after my father buried me and he discovered me in my bedroom with my slit-wrists fully healed, sleeping in my bed as if I never left, he realized I had the SUICIDE AND ETERNITY GENES. He had seen this kind of case once before during his career as a psychiatric surgeon. It rarely appears in the medical literature. Soon thereafter, he went to work on THE IMPLANT. My father is crafty like that—inventing dream-and-nightmare extractors, a fourth-dimensional eye-set for the blind, and a home you can carry in your head. He and I knew he could do it. I thought, at the time, he was working on 'an implant' of stem-cells that would reconstruct the faulty neurons spinning me into suicidal depression. That wasn't it at all. Oh, no. Oh, no..." We get in bed together and we're entwined. I wish we could be like this for months, but by then, I would be filled with the hottest kind of dread. It was coming—all the succubae that I harbor; all my broken necks wanting to snap; and my saliva turning into embalming fluid. But before then, we would finally get naked. My dad thinks I'm bedding down with the prostitute, finally. It's the best he could've hoped for me. No wife, just a bought-for woman. Little does he know I've met my future wife with whom I made the SUICIDE PACT when we were children; and I went so dead, I was siphoned into another universe where I had a slightly different address and my dad had new fingerprints and I was a bit more insane than my first self. I don't remember this woman-as-girl at all, except for those angelic feet—soft and heavenly and smelling of baby powder. We were to be married in death, but instead I was buried and repressed any memory of her. But I'm here and she's here! My child-self is still buried in the grave down the street! My repressed wife, Ellen, has risen from the unconscious—nude, horny with THE IMPLANT that'll cure us both from the cranial resins that fuck up our worldviews. "D," she says. "Let's PROCREATE."

"I'm not ready for children, Ellen."

"Ever since they sanctioned my birth certificate, I've inhabited the name *Ellen*." She unveils her boobs and I'm almost satiated and almost sick. No three teats today! No, sir. They're the normal, beckoning boobs for cavemen that have, since before official history, lured men and some women to salivate and faint. For me, they're only the second set of breasts I've experienced (not counting the three-teats-of-my-hallucinated-wife). The first real ones: a small pair on a girl from childhood whose face and name I have forgotten. With her, too, we had the SUICIDE PACT. And *those* feet...

"Come suckle and PROCREATE, D."

I turn over and recklessly mangle her position, mouthing every inch and nipple like some loon, my cock going obtuse and she doesn't care, she even laughs in a good way and hugs my entire self. "Are you going... to... take off... your panties?" I'm about jumping up and down in need of an exorcism.

"You sure are ready, aren't you, D?"

"Ever since my first penis."

She smiles grandly and it's about forever as she slips off the cotton panties. Come on, come on, I think. Is this a time for fainting? Should I run out of here because vaginas hide banshees? Maybe I should summon a shaman?

"Are you going to show her to me?" I ask, regretting it for sure.

"Of course, silly. It's yours! All yours! I've been waiting for you since you were buried six times."

She teases me by slipping her panties just below her hips.

"Go, goddamn it!" I exclaim because my groin can't stand the tension of a whole life waiting for the sight of WOMANHOOD and all its visceral complications. "Doggy, doggy, doggy, get on the drool with the pimpled tongue of your gentility, your pure-bred licking of the appendages on the perverted owners, my doggy, my pure-bred groin angling to penetrate the crevice of that female!" I'm about to punt my football; I'm about stick my whole self in!

And her panties go down like nothing. It's not like the sunsets, or the romances of cruises, or martinis, or any sex I'd ever imagined. "What is *that*?" I ask, nearly crying.

Ellen spreads out her arms, her face to the side, as if she were in a fashion show unfurling her wings so the audience could savor the entirety of her. You can almost hear the applause, the chairs flying, the men and women zipping out of their lives. Ellen looks between her legs at her numinous, metallic genitals. "D, that's it! It's my IMPLANT! Father operated on me so that, someday, I could give my husband the perfect gift from my genuine soul!"

She frowns at my ghastly expression because she had always imagined her husband mounting her metallic genitals without fright; without hesitance. "D, it's the cure for the SUICIDE AND ETERNITY GENES. Well, officially, it was patented as the 'UTERINE CARBURETOR.' Yes, it's my UTERINE CARBURETOR!"

"Your father really found a cure for melancholy and suicidal depression and implanted you with a UTERINE CARBURETOR?!" My groin is shriveled, but still wants to be loved.

"No, silly, he devised the UTERINE CARBURETOR for the ETERNITY GENE. Now we can do suicides *perfectly* and never, *ever* come back again... It's THE IMPLANT. The answer lies within my UTERINE CARBURETOR."

This truly was her UTERINE CARBURETOR— titanium, radiating, cold as glaciers in the hefts of oceans, sharp, yam-shaped and sticking out from her reddened vaginal opening. There was no way to stick anything in. No way for living. No way for my protu- berance to embrace the damp home inside her. All hope is lost. Sensuality is lost to the history of the 20th century and the many wars we fought to come home to our wide-open wives. This CARBURETOR—this sword with a small, urethra-type opening at the tip of it—is a replication of manliness axed into my girl's vulva. It is not the cure. It's simply the mechanization of *human body memories*. It is the last of our INDUSTRIAL REVOLUTION that began with slavery, sweatshops, savagery, railroads, world wars, and the end of human history. The UTERINE CARBURETOR proves the death of the *God-concept*. People like my father would never understand.

I understand perfectly.

"I was buried six times?" I ask suddenly.

"Really? My father never said anything about that. Sure, I thought I committed suicide successfully, but it was more of a dream than a true belief." I stretch my neck toward the window as if I could see the cemetery from here. She strums her fingers through my thinning hair. This, I like. This is what mothers should do.

"Of course your father wouldn't remember that. Each time you reentered his life, his memory of your grave and headstone slipped away into the ether. I swear there are six headstones with your name on them: D. Ortiz-Thurman. It's *quite* a name, actually. I doubt you would like to visit your bodies, would you?"

Part of me wants to. Part of me wants to exhume my bodies—to see if there are the remnants of brains in my other skulls, but perhaps *that* is what stays with the *living-me*. The rest of my bodies are simply husks and memories and disappearances. "My suicides duplicated my corpses?"

"Let's not speak of death right now, D. We'll have plenty of eternities and solar systems to traverse while dead. We'll be together, then, in an enmeshed kind of way."

Have I really been in this apartment for weeks, for years, or simply one night? Ellen is no longer a woman, or even *Homo sapiens*. She grins as if she were happy and horny and ready for procreation. It's not sex anymore, and never would be again. Here, right here in Ellen's dank apartment, is the beginning of THE NEW HUMANKIND, but that's not the correct description at all. There are no labels for *happenings* when they first rupture through EVOLUTION.

Yet, my appendage still plumps because of its instinct to puncture flesh. It truly has a mind of its own. I desire nothing, and I never will again. My appendage is no longer mine—it belongs to the dustbin of another millennium. "What are we going to do?" I ask, determined to go forward with this experiment. She surely was *not* going to put the titanium CARBU-

RETOR in my bum! I would *never* be raped by a woman and her carburetor, however uterine and womanly it claims to be. "What, Ellen?"

She unveils her breasts as if her upper body belonged to another epoch. We have one foot in the past, one foot in the terrible future. We are evolutionary, human change, and we don't even want to live out our own lives, much less carry the burden of the whole species.

But hers are sumptuous breasts! Her areolas are constellations of campfire nights, meanderings of my boyhood into the woods I wished for. Looking at those breasts—fuck it, call them the *tits* they are—I nearly jump out of my skin with all my lifetime of cum exploding from every orifice of my body. I would drain all of my potential sons and daughters onto her carpet as an omen of what families we could've birthed.

"You're dripping out of your underwear, D. Why don't you just take them off?" I do, and the protuberance is smaller now that it's in the presence of Ellen—an introduction to the world of seduction that no longer exists. The rest of the world doesn't even know it yet. I chuckle out of embarrassment. It's tiny in front of her. Chuckle, chuckle! Guffaw, guffaw!

"It's OK, D. Really, everything will be OK from here on out." She closes the distance between us. I wonder if, finally, she's going to masturbate the shit out of me.

She puts her index finger to my lips. "Just don't breathe," as the metal UTERINE CARBURETOR scolds my thigh coldly—our two protuberances nearly touching, but one more useful than the other. And it's not mine, I know it. "We have to prepare you for your trans-formation."

"Are... you..." and I'm embarrassed as I slink her hand toward my protuberance. "Will... you...?"

She wags her index finger. "I love you, D. I'm no longer capable of that. My vaginal opening is more important than simple pleasures, now. I must tell you, the UTERINE CARBURETOR roots deep into me, past the walls of the uterus itself, into the fallopian tubes—the CARBURETOR roots spindle into delicate spider webs, thinner even, until the roots are the ghosts of webs, and sprout into the structures and molecules of all the ova I ever created. The godly metal has turned my uterus into a LIVING SELF. My uterus that once would give life is now its own LIFE."

I'm frowning. I'm sickened. One's red sex is supposed to be pure sensation and *not* have a cerebellum of its own. Like us deformed humans, her uterus' serotonin, too, is probably all fucked up. Her uterus yearns for dopamine, I bet. Ellen's uterus is suicidal.

Ellen would never *ever* give birth to my ELENA III, even though Ellen loves me so. But I surely couldn't put my protuberance into the opening of her sentient uterus. Its neurons are made of metal. Its dark thoughts surely can't tolerate a protuberance of a deformed, horny, middle-aged man. "What's *my* transformation, then, Ellen?" Fuck it, I will give into whatever she has planned for me. Like Ellen said: *We will commit suicides perfectly and desperately.* I put my underwear back on. She traipses around with her tits flailing. Even in front of the window, she dances. She's excited to be asexual. Her transformation is nearly complete. Now, of course, it depends upon me. All things defiled depend on D—the most unlikely of men.

"Go home now, D. Go home, sleep, and take in this birth of our new, suicidal marriage. Father will be coming out of his cube to prepare for *your* surgery. It's been many years since he implanted my UTERINE CARBURETOR. Now, he will program his robotic, assistant surgeon to perform the implantation in you." She frowns. "I'm sorry, D. I got so excited! I didn't even ask if you'd consent to your IMPLANT. Will you, D, will you?" Her eyebrows are desperate. Every inch of her sweaty flesh beckons for my reply because her perfected suicide, for whatever unknown fucking reason, depends upon me.

"Sure," I say, slipping a piece of grape-flavored gum into my maw. I love grape-flavored gum because it reminds me of the sad treasures of watching cartoons when my mother suffered six-feet-deep in her grave. "If it means we'll die *for real* together and it'll stop my corpse from duplicating. A man needs only one grave, one corpse, and one life. The noose at age twelve wasn't enough for this nincompoop." But then, I remember my beloved, immigrant father. His homeland is far away—so far away, his D has no idea where it lies on the map of our Earth. I sigh and slouch. Nothing is perfect. There are no perfect solutions.

Exhumations

For the first time in my life, I feel guilty for wanting to kill myself. I realize I do, in fact, love my dad. His English is so accented it makes me want to weep. Maybe it's not the accent; it's the symbol of him that brings out my love for the man. He is a real dude—a human of our ancient history. No metallic protuberances for him! He gave birth to me even though his wife hated the essence of her own son and killed herself during childbirth! I'm his only son, his only offspring who has fucked-up serotonin, but will propel THE NEW HUMANKIND into the hot beast of our world! No more arcane sex, arcane brains, arcane sons for the new millennium. No, all humans will be imbued with SUICIDE GENES. Their cells will kill themselves. There will be no more wavering before the offing of the SELF. It'll be totally natural. It will define our new age.

Dad, I love you, even though I'll devastate you once again. But it's better this way. You'll never bury your son again, and then forget about burying him for the sixth or seventh time, but you'll remember me in your nightmares. I'll be over and done with. That will be it. You will eat breakfast and drink coffee in peace. And please, make love to your woman. Hold her tightly. This is your last forever.

I open the door to my home. Ellen's hermit, psychiatric surgeon of a father is preparing my IMPLANT as I enter my home. Dad is at the table with his coffee. He turns toward me and nearly cries. "Where have you been all night, D?"

Has it only been one night? I look down at myself and realize I'm wearing my funeral suit.

Suddenly in shock, I say, "I've been with a woman, Ellen."

"The prostitute?"

"No, that's Aida, but I've divorced her. I have a

new woman, Ellen." I lower my head in guilt. I feel the inexpensive material of my funeral suit. My suit will be the skin of my eternity and I'll be soaked in blood.

"Ellen," he says, "Ellen." I know what he's thinking: another *Elena*. He must think I've truly gone insane having invented yet *another* Elena. But this one isn't my fault. Ellen is the fault of her own father.

"I thought, maybe..." And he can't get himself to say it. "D, son, I simply couldn't bare it again. Promise me. Right now, before God, that you will *never* do it again. If you embraced Jesus Christ, perhaps it would help you from suffering so badly."

I walk up to him and hug his shoulders. *Jesus can't help me*, I'm about to say. But who am I to take away his savior? We should all have a savior. But I was born with a genetic mutation. I can *live forever* even though that's the last thing I *want* to do. I live in a dilemma. Perhaps religion would've helped me if my mother had loved my soul. I kiss my dad's forehead.

He tries to push me away because men don't embrace each other in this fashion. He gives in, though, as I keep my damp lips on his forehead. "Go to church with me, D. There are nice girls there."

I back away and smile. "I think I found my wife. Besides, I told you I don't want to date the retarded girl. I may be crazy, but I won't date a retarded girl."

He lowers his head. I know it's not his intent to introduce me to the mentally challenged girl. I heard she's hot, though, and brunette, but has the thoughts of felines. Dad simply wants me to believe in something, to live, to endure.

"It's not in the cards, Dad," I say as I walk upstairs toward my odiferous bedroom.

"Next time, leave a note!" he yells.

I lie in bed and it's suddenly very early in the morning. Not even the televisions in our neighbors' apartments are on. I've been in a daze all night. That year with Ellen was only *one night*—last night. I met her at the funeral yesterday and we were married and now we will give birth to our suicides. Ah, rubbish! It's all a delusion of mine. Like I said—when I'm depressed I want to be even more depressed until I relish it like a wife. It's awful when you're in love with a demented emotion. It's an animal that hunkers down inside me. Perhaps it's a badger, but it's probably a mole. Or, it's Ellen. That's dumb and far too symbolic. Ellen lives down the street and her father is sharpening his knives as we speak and programming his robot to perform the surgery and the sutures. What will I look like? What will they implant in me? Hopefully, not a badger or a mole. I don't like rabid wildlife for shit.

I reach under my bed for the noose I secretly twined those short weeks ago. It's not identical to the twelve-year-old boy's, but it will do. I pull it on top of my bulbous body as if I could love it and desire it and feel it. But it's the *effect* that I yearn for, not *the-thing-in-itself*. Rope can exact muscular abrasions upon the flesh, but *not* to be mistaken for the grazes of lust—*and which will never come to fruition for this impotent beast!* Rope connotes *passion*, definitely, but it's the passion of molten, murderous rock—bowels and minds doing the whirly dervish in free-fall—until the rope catches short and stunts my growth. That's the *felt-for-pain* which will shatter Dad's spirit through his bed and through his sleep. Perhaps, he'll boycott sleeping from then on out, but I will always fall free—down, down—dazed and getting more zany every fucking eon after all of my lunatic clothes burn off and I'm nude with the asteroids, comets, space flotsam, severed angels, and the vastness of the vacuous mind that space is, and even my piss and diarrhea coagulate into globules of the loneliest waste. I'll never wipe away my shit again. I'll wish, for once in my entire life, to be covered with my own bowel movements. But this is the predicament I've created for me—mistaking death for the *end-of-it-all*, but perhaps (and I won't know it until

I know) this is the *epitome* of all HUMAN
EXPERIENCE—the way white embodies all colors and all
light. My bowels and its minds will embody all
darkness because I insisted on swallowing my noose
and my devils whole. As I lie here, the noose calling my
monosyllabic name, I'll go through with it nonetheless.
Fuck all the warnings and what-ifs, even if it all comes
true. I am doomed to try my hand at magic. Yes, Ellen
and I are destined for the free fall of eternity and outer
space. We will hold hands in absolute terror—but only
if Ellen is truly my wife; and if she even exists; and if
she is not actually the Mommy who hates me so.

That's when you have to sever the rope and the
cord.

I lie here, finally out of the suicidal daydream,
and dressed in my funeral suit. The fucking funeral suit
made from cheap material. When did I put on my
funeral suit?

I open my shirt and, hell, THE IMPLANT's already
inside me! I wondered what it would look like, and
there it *is* stabbing me—titanium like Ellen's
CARBURETOR, but protruding from where my belly-
button used to be. It's called the UMBILICAL
RECEPTOR—yes, somehow I do know that. Don't ask me
how I know this. It's in most of the classified
psychiatric literature, but I've been a professional
mental patient my whole life. I'm pretty much
theoretical. I'm schooled in all the sicknesses and the
devilish cures. Ellen and her father's robotic surgical
assistant must've climbed up my stairs this night,
punctured my tummy, stuffed the RECEPTOR in *deeply*,
and that's why I was in such a daze because of their
savage anesthesia. I stand up to stare at my UMBILICAL
RECEPTOR in the mirror. I happen to look out the
window as well and catch a glimpse of Elena II kissing
her gargantuan boyfriend, still in his fur coat. It still
hurts to know that she loves him, not me, but I have
Ellen now and she's perfect for me. Goodbye to all the

old wives from the past! Ellen and I are our own INDUSTRIAL REVOLUTION. And I know what the RECEPTOR, indeed, is *for*. For once, I put two-and-two together. Two-and-two—like badger and deerskin sewn together at the cranium to forge a hybrid animal we all *loved* as children. Kiddies love centaurs, gods with lightning bolts in their heads, two-brained monsters, murderers with six hands and six feet, but mostly they love the parents who save them from their imagination. Most children outgrow their devotion to sewing together disparate skins. My UMBILICAL RECEPTOR protrudes from the slit in my stomach where my belly-button once was, and yet I have outgrown nothing. I'm actually growing *in*.

I waddle downstairs and Dad is already finishing the caffeine. "What a night, Dad." He barely looks up, and keeps sipping. He's wearing a different colored fedora this grand morning. "Did you leave any coffee for me?" I ask.

"I thought you were dead," he says, slurping the black juice. And then he looks up. "I'm sorry, son. I didn't mean it. I really didn't." He frowns and looks at his feet as if forgiveness lay between his toes. "I swear."

I yawn, jump off the last step and pat Dad on his back. "No prob, old dude. I thought I was dead, too. It's a miracle." *There's a whole cemetery dedicated to me*, I almost exclaim. That would be arrogant, because my corpses couldn't form a whole platoon of dead soldiers. They certainly don't deserve any patriotism.

"Yeah, it is." He grasps my hand in his. This is my family—these two decrepit hands. They're both so veined. Shit, I can hardly distinguish mine from his. It must be the lotion he uses religiously. Or, maybe it's religion itself. "Glad to have you here, D."

He knows nothing of the UMBILICAL RECEPTOR or what will go *in*. Even I don't know that. If he did know, he would certainly prescribe the anti-psychotics to cure me of the cord. The doctor cut me loose of the afterbirth once and screwed up my circumcision—no one needs to do that again. *But, Dad,* I would say, *this here is no cord or afterbirth. You might say it's the beginning of the universe. If you look in, through my bowels and its minds, you might catch a glimpse of the Big Bang.*

"Glad to have you, too, Dad."

This embrace. This love.

I'm about to walk away, when I stumble and fall on all fours. I can't feel my left leg, arm or hand. I didn't think it would end this way! A stroke! Come on, now! "Ugh," I mutter.

"Are you okay, D? It must be the MULTIPLE SCLEROSIS. Have you been taking your medication? D?" He reaches for the numb side of my body, as if I were cut in two.

"Since when did I have MULTIPLE SCLEROSIS? Are you insane?"

He looks into my eyes the way only a parent can. But he has blue fucking eyes! And he says I have MULTIPLE SCLEROSIS!

"Dad," I say, "when did you turn German?"

"Come on, get up," he says. "I know you haven't been taking your medication. Do I have to do everything for you? You're making yourself sick! Sicker than you already are." He furrows his brow and it scares me. I may get a whipping.

I sit up on the couch and my limbs tingle. I begin to have double-vision. I see two Dads where there should only be one. I thought I was simply a mental patient. And now my dad's German! "Dad, where are you from?"

He sits next to me and insists on clapping on my numb leg. "I'm from the same small town where I met your mother, D. Like I've always told you. You don't remember anything. You'd like to think we were simple people, peasants or refugees. I'd like to think we're the children of the Lord."

"But you're friggin' German, now."

"Ha! And it's not like you don't speak Aramaic, too." He smiles and his blue eyes terrify me. I've changed him. My actions have reassigned his body and heritage.

"I have to go, Dad."

"You need to go to the doctor? You're scheduled for this week, but I can call him and schedule something sooner." He tips his fedora toward the back of his head as if there's nothing to worry about. He's been dealing with my crises his whole life.

I get up, straighten my suit pants, button my shirt incorrectly, and stumble toward the door. "I have to see Ellen, Dad. Please, let me see Ellen." I walk and open the front door, not wearing any shoes or socks.

"What Ellen?!" he screams as I close the door on him.

***

"God, I didn't think you'd come back, D." Ellen helps me onto her couch. "You look like hell."

"Well, what do you expect with you and your father's robotic surgical assistant coming into my bedroom to perform a non-sterile operation on my belly? Didn't you think I'd get an infection or something?"

"D, we did the surgery here under the most sterile of conditions. My father invented a new kind of sterility; more sterile than a vacuum. You just didn't clean it like you were supposed to." She examines the UMBILICAL RECEPTOR and the flesh around it. "It actually looks fine, D. Do you have some other kind of sickness or something?" She puts her maternal hands on her hips. What's up with all the scolding today?

"Dad says I have MULTIPLE SCLEROSIS." I lie on the couch like a toad about to implode. "I'm not so sure about that."

"You don't know if you have MULTIPLE SCLEROSIS? This could jeopardize us, D." She sits next to me and wipes away the sweat beads from my elderly forehead. "But we can't wait. Either we're going to do this, or we're not." Her damned nipples are erect. If she's asexual now, why are her nipples teasing me like that? Don't they have any compassion for a man whose sex has been completely rationed?

"Let's fucking do it," I say, trying to stand up. I limp around in a circle and plop back down on the couch. "I don't even know what we're doing, anyway." I stare at her nipples getting harder, harder. "I think my dad turned German."

"It's not impossible," she says, like she's talking about a caterpillar turning into a moth. She smiles and I love her. Really, I do. Why do we have to be so suicidal all the time? Couldn't we simply hang out, watch movies and chomp on turkey jerky? What would be so wrong with that?

"Look, Ellen, I don't know about you, but I've never been asexual and never will be. Your... vaginal opening... is, well, filled with titanium. I can see how that would hamper your arousal. But my appendage is OK, despite the botched circumcision. I just have a RECEPTOR in my belly." I want her to unzip me, take it in her mouth, swallow me up, but no, we're destined for the noose. Always, the noose. If only I weren't such an addict for death-wishes, I would be a regular American.

"It'll never be the same, D." She covers her breasts as if she's embarrassed by her natural beauty.

"It never *was*. Period." I open my shirt because I know that's what I'm supposed to do. Even in my death and my mechanical sexing, I'm simply a man-prostitute. "Do with me what you'd like," I tell her.

"Lie on the floor, D."

"Is it good for a person with MULTIPLE SCLEROSIS to lie on their backs on hard ground?"

"You don't have that. Believe me." She takes off

her pants and panties and the titanium madness sticks out from between her thighs and it hums! I'm serious! It hums! "Can you hear it, D? My UTERINE CARBURETOR has invented a language for my uterus! I almost want to name it, right, D?" She wears this beguiling grin. There's something satanic about all of this. I can't put my finger on it, but there's definitely a devilish hue here.

"Well?" I ask.

Ellen climbs on top of me with her titanium appendage—rooted deep into her ova and her very essence—and she's trying to finagle it. You see, this is her first penis. Aw, isn't that so cute? "Scoot down," she says, taking aim at my UMBILICAL RECEPTOR. How could I not have known that this was going to happen? *She's* going to impregnate *me*? But that doesn't make any sense. Wasn't the whole point to do some visceral newly invented sex to cure our ETERNITY GENES so we could rapidly die in due course? When did impregnation come into the mix?

"You're going to get me pregnant?" I ask Ellen.

She swipes away her lustful swaths of hair from her sweaty face. "No, D, come on. I explained this to you and you signed the disclaimer for my father. Well, actually, for my father's robotic surgical assistant, but no matter." She spits a bit of hair from her mouth. I can tell she's frustrated. I would be, too, if I were a woman trying to maneuver my first titanium penis.

"Explain it to me again," I say. I'm in a studious mood. My erection is long gone. That will never happen again. But I do feel my UMBILICAL RECEPTOR open and close it's tiny, urethral maw. I have control over this animal. This metal has truly come to life.

"D, I'm giving you part of my body. It's like a communion. One body into the next—from Ellen into D. The UTERINE CARBURETOR translates the stem cells of my uterus to be harvested in you. You know, like when a surgeon transplants a piece of someone's liver into the ill patient, and it grows, replicating itself into a new liver? But that's 20th century thinking. The CARBURETOR is simply transmitting uterine *information* into you through your RECEPTOR. It's code, D. It's *language*."

"So, I'm going to have a tiny piece of your uterine information in my belly?"

She sighs loudly now. "Jesus. D, my uterus will grow in you to transmit my NEW GENETIC MATERIAL. We'll become one, D. Don't you remember? In your dream? When I entered your dream?"

"I don't remember anything anymore." I sniffle. If I had a mommy, I'd cry for her right now. This is the point in my life when it would've been advantageous to have been breast-fed. Breast milk has a curative effect on the suicidal infant. Instead, I have titanium, stem cells, and the possibility of this woman's uterine information festering in me. "Well," I say, "how are we going to die if we're both pregnant?"

Ellen almost collapses. "Ugh, D. We'll have NEW AGE UTERUSES, but we won't be pregnant, for Christ's sake. Our UTERUSES or UTERI or whatever will simply be vessels for our replenished SUICIDE GENES. Our SUICIDE GENES need to split, divide and conquer and live inside each of us in order for this experiment to succeed. It's a uterine means-to-an-end, D. *The* end! I mean, do you really want to fucking live forever killing yourself for the rest of eternity?"

I think of my noose when I was twelve years old. I was a naïve boy. I was sad. Rope seemed so simple then. Death was not complicated. "I guess I don't want to kill myself for the rest of my life." I pout because all I wanted all my life, besides suicide, was to get truly laid. "Where's your father during all of this anyway?" I ask, dumbfounded.

"Well, D, can I just stick it in?!"

The Morning After

I wake up in my own bed, no longer in my funeral suit. I'm wearing dirty underwear, a yellowed t-shirt and black socks. Why am I wearing dress socks to bed? I yawn because it's a lovely, sunny morning. Dad will be percolating some caffeine before too long. Maybe *I'll* make it this time. He's done enough for me. So I get up, and my left leg collapses again. Goddamned MULTIPLE SCLEROSIS or UTERINE RECEPTOR infection! Maybe I have some new, metallic venereal disease. I go into the bathroom to take a good, long morning leak. I lift up my t-shirt and notice the RECEPTOR is no longer there in my gut. There's simply a deeply reddened scar where some debauched doctor sewed me up. The belly-button is gone, too. It's as if I was never connected to a placenta in the first place. The UTERINE INFORMATION, SUICIDE GENES, Aramaic, my German dad, to hell with it all! I'm just good old D—schizoid, depressed, and, I guess, with MULTIPLE SCLEROSIS. Maybe Ellen killed herself and I chickened out this time. That would serve her right for betraying me when I was twelve and hung myself and, well, I don't even remember anything about her except those angelic feet.

I look in the mirror and, at first, I think I have broken out with horrible acne. Actually, it's simply one bulbous red pimple on my right temple. It looks like a scabbed-over exit wound. Oh God, that would be a new one! I raise my index finger to rub the outer rim of the burgundy indentation. It actually feels quite wonderful. The ragged hole in my head is tingly and ultra-sensitive. I rub and rub and, yet again, I've discovered a new kind of sex. Listen, ladies and gentlemen, here before you is a man with an inverted penis in his head! Rub it right and it, too, will speak. But what kind of cuss does the hole dribble out? My guess, it's simpleton, hooker speak since the soul the wound leads to is highly deformed. But it's not dead yet! The reddened exit-wound is nicely orgasmic. This cannot be a coincidence. There are no coincidences in my world of the sexually rationed. Who wouldn't want to jerk off a new hole in your head while people look on—disgusted—and think you're simply scraping out a wound? OK, maybe I simply have semen backed up into my cerebellum that any orifice—even an apparent gunshot—takes on the hue of the sexual and absurd. Dad would never believe this one.

So I limp downstairs and my dad is wearing a wig and sipping tea. I'm stunned! Kicked in the gullet! Has my dad gone transvestite? Has he finally gone mad and joined my peculiar race? "Dad, why the hell are you wearing a wig?" Hobble, hobble. "Since when you do you drink friggin' tea?" Hobble.

"Don't play games with me, boy," the person exclaims as it turns its ham-hock head toward me. "You call me *Dad* one more time and I'll smack the shit out of you like I should've done when you were born. *Mother* is my name. *Mother!*"

Hobble, fuck, I nearly pass out! My blood has truly gone psychotic having reinvented Mommy in the body of my dad who is now wearing a wig and impersonating his wife while bespeaking the kind of evil of a child molester! I need Mommy like I need a hole in my head, even if I *do* have a hole in my head that's not quite a hole, but really a deepening, sensuous indentation. But that's not important. I'm meeting Mommy for the first time and she has proved that she *does* hate me. Well, even if it's really Dad siphoning the dead-speech of his wife. Language comes out wrangled and mutated when siphoned from zombies. The worst kind of random cuss comes out of a parental medium, particularly when the father's a vessel for his dead wife and he's dressed like a transvestite that drinks the blood and saliva of terrorized children. Dead people and parents make the worst hookers.

I hobble toward the MOMMY—who is somehow taller than the previous morning when she was Dad, but bulbous in the tummy. Or maybe I should just say it's *obese*. The stomach protrudes horizontally—not in an evenly shaped sphere. Whatever, you say, but it's important, but I can't tell you why. I heave and sit on the carpet. My left face is sulking, or sinking, or simply going fucked. My whole body is slipping asymmetrical with illness. Like Dad said (wherever he is or if he's the MOMMY now), I may have the MULTIPLE SCLEROSIS. He even explained that I've had the illness all my life! That's ridiculous because I would've taken note of something like that roaming through my body and mind.

"Get off the floor, you no-good nincompoop!" The MOMMY with the fright-wig and five o'clock shadow wags its finger at me like all threatening adults do in 1950s movies. What I *don't* see coming is the whack on the side of my head with a wooden spoon!

"Jesus! Dad? Mother? What did I do but simply get sick and go on the disability?" I cover my head to protect me not only from pain, but to cover the open hole in my temple that leads straight to my mind—can't have the MOMMY violating me in such an intimate way, however accidentally.

And then the MOMMY opens its legs wide, still erect and standing, and out from under its homely dress plops out a bloody mass of wretchedness or barbecue or ruined cow. "Damn it, you see that, boy?! I'm consistently and forever dropping afterbirths ever since you were born!" It bends over and picks up the bloody mass with its bare hands and heaps the mulch into the sink. The MOMMY turns on the garbage disposal which makes sounds like deathly banana peels going through—thick and stopping up the garbage disposal blades with spittle and blood and globules leaping out from the drain. The MOMMY pays the afterbirth no mind. It's not that I want to turn away, it's that I *must*. No living being should have to witness their own placenta going straight down into the wreckage and underbelly of this haunted town.

The MOMMY walks toward me and about yells into my ear—the dying one.

And then the phone rings. As the MOMMY answers, there's much manly, garbled speech on the other end and the MOMMY wipes its bloodied hands on its homely dress and it simply nods. It's broken by the man on the other end. Someone has actually broken it. I wish I could break it and split its spine, but it's a miracle I'm awake and not incontinent lying here on the dirty carpet. The MOMMY hangs up the phone.

"That's it! Your father exclaimed that you have the MRI scheduled and we must take you to the MRI, so get dressed in your funeral suit, boy, because I'm driving you as quickly as I can to the hospital to stuff you into the MRI machine to take pictures of your freaky brain. I'm not sure why your father insists on this, but he yelled at me over the cellular phone while he screeched down the street on his way to the hospital and that his son *is* an emergency. I don't respond well to emergencies, so I guess I should've wakened you earlier and not smacked you with the wooden spoon since the emergency must be in your head and that could've screwed things up between me and your father if you were to slip into a coma like you're prone to do." The MOMMY clears its throat and massages the five o'clock shadow. "Go, then, D, jump into your funeral suit so we can lead you through your emergency so dying doesn't commence and so father won't get angry with me."

"Can you help me up... Mommy?" I lend her my veined right hand—the good one. She weakly pulls me to my feet and I hobble up the stairs. Should I iron the suit first? The MOMMY watches me as I pull my heft up the stairs and into the bedroom until I close the door shut. My suit is laid out perfectly on my perfectly made bed. It's as if my UNCONSCIOUS prepared for my crisis all along. I won't question this too much, so I climb as best I can into the suit. The left face and left body are weakening quickly. This may be the last of any evenness, whatever that means. I *do* feel the UMBILICAL RECEPTOR trying to puncture through my abdomen. I thought I got rid of that thing! Fucking metallic parasite! Anyway, this is no time to ponder the meaning and causes of this illness—whether SCLEROSIS or mania or laziness or metallic or venereal. My body is simply giving up, at least my left body is. Shit, this is an emergency! Dad will be angry if I'm late to my own crisis; if the wigged MOMMY downstairs hasn't dismembered him already.

The MOMMY speeds through alleyways, freeways, boulevards, and even a lawn, and scrapes sidewalks—hubcaps sparking and me in a tight panic. My left head hurts and must be suffering migraines and paralysis. I imagine my dad's wrong—I don't remember any diagnosis of the MULTIPLE SCLEROSIS. But then again, I didn't know my dad wore wigs and pretended to be the MOMMY. Either that or the MOMMY is a hired actor/actress playing the role of Mommy and doing a horrible job or maybe a great one since I didn't actually know Mommy during my lifetime. My guess is this is a kidnapping, but I'm middle-aged which makes me kind of pathetic, but I was smacked with a wooden spoon, am dead in my left body, and have a slowly opening wound on my right temple that's begun to ooze. I see the MOMMY in the rearview mirror and it may be driving with its eyes closed. It's better if I don't know these things since I own this crisis. Zig and zag, almost destroying a freeway barrier, many drivers enraged and cursing at our vehicle, a gun going off, the MOMMY gripping the steering wheel with all its strength and it starts to rain. I look out the side window and our tires are beginning to smoke and peel. That's never a good sign. "Hey, parent, I think we're going to blow a tire." I'm more concerned that my speech is beginning to sound fat-lipped and retarded because my left body is asleep and I'm partially asleep and awake and afraid. That doesn't stop me from observing that we're about to blow out all of our tires. I don't want to go to Heaven with this MOMMY.

"Shut up, boy!" the supposed MOMMY shouts without looking at me. It even pushes the gas pedal down further. "This is my womb and we're pushing your birth to the limit!" it exclaims as we penetrate a dimly lit tunnel. I listen to the wheels thump against the uneven pavement and the echoes of our driving and I can see trees and skyscrapers and a whole new city at the opening of the tunnel in front of us. We're almost there if we don't die. The light shines over us as we exit the echoes of the tunnel, and for some reason I'm at peace as if warm milk had been poured over my flimsy and fat body. I hate the taste of warm milk, especially when it gets a skin, but it feels wonderful draping over the fatness.

The hospital. Emergency room entrance. We screech and halt suddenly and with distinction. The doctors, smokers, and fecund patients all look at us. The MOMMY with its uneven, bulbous stomach rushes through the automatic sliding glass doors having forgotten about me—the owner of this crisis, at least according to my dad if he's actually still alive and he's not the MOMMY. I open my door and bumble out like a drunken Chaplin without a cool cane and almost trip on my face. No one comes to my aid. I don't even think they noticed. Many rushed in and followed the MOMMY as if it was having a heart attack or a baby.

Finally, I make it through the emergency room doors. I notice the MOMMY lying on a gurney, leaning forward, and the staff is yelling, "Don't push just yet! Hold on, Miss! Just hold on!" What a coincidence that it drove me to the hospital as I was having an attack of the brain and it was actually pregnant. Does that mean I'll have a sibling at middle-age? Not likely, since either I've been kidnapped or Dad hired this loon for some ungodly reason or Dad is pregnant over there.

But I spot my father down the hallway and he comes running after me. "What the hell? I came to the house to pick you up after you called me and you weren't there?" I notice his fedora on the hallway floor.

"Someone's going to crush your hat," I tell him with a Novocain speech impediment.

"Where did you go? I told you to stay put. You know that when you get sick, you have a tendency to wander around. I should've never left you." He and some nurses help me onto a gurney and my left face is about to flop off. "At your age..." Dad says.

"The person you hired to play the MOMMY drove me here. Besides, I'm middle-aged, Dad. I can take care of myself." Dad has a perplexed look as if he were seeing me for the first time in his life. Maybe I'm an imposter as well. Someone hired me to play me, but I'm not recognized *as* me.

But then Dad says, "*How* did you get here?"

"Over there, the MOMMY is giving birth to me or some other stillborn." I point to a curtained room where all you can hear is moaning and the hushed sorrows of young doctors and interns.

"Is he normally this way?" the nurse with the tight booty asks my dad.

"Not this bad. No, not this bad." Dad's English has improved since I saw him last. Perhaps he's practiced his English in the last twenty-four hours. I forget what language he grew up speaking. I want to say Latin, but I do recall something about Aramaic and Spanglish all mixed into a mud hut or whatever. Dad looks at me. "What next?" he asks the nurse. I actually catch him glancing at the nurse's butt and I'm deeply proud, but also embarrassed. The nurse doesn't seem to mind, given the state of my left face and left body.

"What's he suffering from?" she asks my dad.

He mumbles.

"What's his diagnosis again?"

He mumbles again.

"Hello? I'm right here," I exclaim through the cotton of my numb lips. "If I were a woman, I'd be approaching menopause. You can direct your questions to me." But I give up and just lay my heavy head on the gurney. It has one of those disposable pillows that aren't very comfortable.

"Doctor?" the nurse exclaims, interrupting the gait of an old dude in a lab coat. She explains something to him and he looks perturbed.

"Yes, an MRI with contrast STAT. Check him for any trauma just in case. Keep me updated." The doctor speeds away barely having looked at me.

And who is being sped through the emergency room doors? It's Ellen! I wasn't sure she even existed anymore. Goddamn! "Ellen!" I yell trying to lift my failing head. "It's me! D!"

She's hooked up to an IV, but does manage to lift her head a bit. "D," I hear her mumble, even from here. She reaches out to me with her pasty hand as if I were right there, right beside her. Wait. What's wrong with *her*? When I left her, she was fine. Sure, she did insert the UTERINE CABURETOR into me and all that, but I'm the one with the MULTIPLE SCLEROSIS. The doctors push her gurney past mine. She can't be more then pre-pubescent, but I do have double-vision right now. As she passes me, she puckers her lips as if to kiss my breath and exhales, "It worked. The UTERINE BINARY CODE was a success, D. No more ETERNITY GENE... and we almost had fun doing it. We kept our pact like we said we would." And her head plops down as her PARENTAL FIGURE suggests that she hush.

Her PARENT is crying for Ellen. It's not her father, though. It's definitely female. The renowned psychiatric surgeon must still be in his cube. A success,

I guess. Really?

And now they're rushing me down the hallway and I can see the fluorescent lights above me swishing by in a stream of consciousness. Is it true? I don't remember going through with anything except THE NEW INTERCOURSE which was quite uninteresting, actually. Damn it! I did want to hug Ellen even though she looked too young for a middle-aged man like me to be hugging, but my double-vision is playing tricks on me, and the MULTIPLE SCLEROSIS has gotten the best of my left face and left body, but Ellen was—is—my wife! Well, almost, anyway. We spent months together, although it may have been one, long night of passion; rationed lust; UTERINE CARBURETOR AND UMBILICAL RECEPTOR COUPLING; implantation of Ellen's UTERINE BINARY CODE into me; and me translating Ellen's UTERINE BINARY CODE into a burgeoning, living organ of my own. I guess stem cells, etc., understand language no matter the source (tongue, liver, uterus, or spine, etc). Somehow, according to Ellen, this NEW INTERCOURSE would extinguish each of our ETERNITY GENES and we wouldn't live in limbo any longer, nor would we duplicate our corpses or our funerals. How does that work? I'm not sure. But as they say, more will be revealed.

I reach up to the deepening indentation in my right temple and rub it gently with my middle finger. Although it's sensitive and is still somewhat arousing, it's mostly painful now. I keep going at it because men are that way (trying not to let anyone in on what I'm doing to myself during my own emergency) and notice blood on my finger. Kind of a lot of it. Kind of deep and thick and almost brown. Oh, man. Now what? And I already miss Ellen if it's true about us being successful. Actually, I feel like weeping.

I've wasted many adulthoods and destroyed many fathers through my bouts of weeping. Each duplicate of my corpse inverted the genetic structure of my father, giving him blue eyes, then violet, and back to brown, and I don't even know what color now. Does he wear glasses at this point? It's possible. He even started wearing a different-colored fedora and sleeping on his right side instead of his left; turned ambidextrous; turned clumsy; but he never turned mean and never forgot my name: D. He did go Deutsch on me, but that may have been a dream. And suddenly Ellen's angelic feet flit into my head and I can almost smell them. What feet, what femininity! Why did our lust for death have to go and muck it all up? I mean, if we truly do have the ETERNITY GENE, would it have been so bad to traipse around the Earth's equator for the rest of time together as husband and wife—or at least until the sun exploded—even if we did duplicate our corpses and committed suicide every now and then? Who really cares if we have multiple coffins and headstones? Is it really that sacrilegious? We are so stupid and so nearly young.

They wheel me into the MRI room. They must've undressed me during all that ruminating because I'm in a gown. I hope they couldn't smell my underwear. My father sits not too far away and makes the sign of the cross over his heart, then waves to me. "He doesn't have any metal on him, does he?" the technician asks. My father shakes his head. I'm lying on the MRI tray. The technician hovers above me. He reeks of cheap aftershave. "Here," he says and realizes I can't grip anything. He puts earplugs in my ears and doesn't seem to notice the hole in my head. "It's going to be very loud in there. But you've done this before, right? Just try not to move and try not to swallow. Here," and he puts a red button attached to a cable on my lap. "This is an emergency button. Just in case. Ready?" He pushes me into the MRI machine. Have I done this before? I sure don't remember. Maybe the technician has me mixed up with some other middle-aged man. At first, it's kind of dark and I can nearly hear my thoughts. *Don't swallow*, I tell myself. Wait. Did the technician ask my father if I had metal on me? Shit, not on me but *in* me! They don't know about the UMBILICAL RECEPTOR. Maybe it doesn't matter since it did retract into my belly or my mind or whatever. Jesus. I hope I don't catch on fire. That's definitely not part of the plan if there *is* any plan. I do begin to tear up. Will I ever see Ellen again? We've been friends since I killed myself when I was twelve! Although I don't remember her from my childhood, her feet were well-known to my spirit and my body once I reunited with her, and I took to her adulthood right away as if we truly were soul-mates in life and in despondency. And the MRI humming starts. Then, there are gigantic mechanical blips and bleeps; blues and greens and yellows all around me; and tremors and noises I can't recognize. How am I supposed to stay still and not swallow during this entire ruckus?

And everything goes absolutely and enormously calm for me. For a second, I think I'm a loony stuffed animal, but no, I'm actually human. Amidst the blips and the bleeps and the crazy lights, I've become very, very calm. I think it must be this Buddha thing, lying here absolutely still encased in a casket-like tube. Is it Buddha's touch I feel? Or perhaps it's the electro-magnetic waves penetrating my head, my heart, my spine, my limbic brain and spirit that's doing the trick. Whatever it is, I realize for the first time in my life that it's possible to feel utterly *even* and *free*. I *do* want to live. I want it desperately and without any reservations whatsoever. Is this all it takes—an emergency and encasement in a casket-like tube with electromagnetic waves swimming through me?

A voice drifts from out of the ceiling of the MRI tube: "Just a few more minutes now. You OK in there?" Is it Buddha, or laughable God, or Rod Serling, or Allen Ginsberg? I hope it's not Ginsberg because he sucks. I know! It's HAL from *2001: A Space Odyssey*! Man meets himself and giant babies and death!

"HAL?" I respond. "Is it you? Am I inside an antagonistic computer? Did I do something wrong?"

"Son?" the voice asks. "You OK? It's just me, the technician."

"Oh," I say, embarrassed. "I'm fine," I tell him. That Neanderthal I saw before I jumped into the noose at age twelve must *not* have been God at all. Or if it was, God, too, has evolved—first into MATTER, now into LIGHT. Wow, it's like being on drugs except I feel absolutely lucid, clear, and surrounded by something akin to *love*. That *is* kind of creepy for a man to say, but it's true. Being *inside* is the epicenter of my entire life.

The MRI ends and the technician takes me out. "That wasn't so bad, was it?" he asks. His aftershave doesn't bother me so much in my state of bliss. I would have squished myself into a microwave if I had known I could feel like this. When I'm suicidal, I crave suicide and swim in the limbs and torsos of my limbic, suicidal reflexes, but for the first time ever, I can't even remember suicide or fathom the idea of taking a nosedive straight through Hell. How could one fathom doing *that*? Ludicrous, I say! There are meadows and puppies and daisies to live for, but also boobs and erections and secretions and feminine body odor and even UTERINE BINARY CODE, as long as you don't let your prick translate too much of *that* diary. I've been touched by the hand of a real God. I'm embarrassed, yes. Dad was right the whole time. Well, not totally. His church doesn't emit electromagnetic waves or house a casket-like encasement where you can get your Buddha on. You never know—that holy water could emit wavelengths. I still wouldn't drink that stuff, but no one insists that you do. Whatever it is, it's not God I want, but the *God-effect*. And isn't that why He gave us skin and genitals? I reach up with my living right hand and gently touch the outer edge of my head wound. Yup! It really is a clitoris or some alien nervous system!

If I could just regain the use of my left face and left body, I'd stroll out of my emergency with my dad in hand, straight into the park to finally meet his old lady, Lydia. I'd even learn a phrase or two of his native tongue. I'd look up my dad's homeland on a gas station map or the internet. Give it time, I tell myself, as they wheel me into a silent, white room with loneliness spray-painted all over the walls.

The curtain is drawn. Ha! It's almost time for the show to start! I can see the silhouettes of the actors—Dad, Nurse, Doctor, Passerby. At least we ditched the PARENTAL FIGURE, right? Maybe they strangled her with her umbilical cord. She was a real drag. Why was it in my house anyway? No matter now. Fuck wigs made from real human hair! I perk up and try to hear what the main actors are saying behind the hospital curtain as the show is finally about to begin.

DAD: What is it? Is it serious?

DOCTOR: I'm afraid so.

NURSE: We're sorry.

DAD: He was always troubled. They told me it was the MULTIPLE SCLEROSIS. Right, Doctor?

DOCTOR: They must've made a... mistake. Or, perhaps it was simply too early to tell.

NURSE: We're truly, truly sorry.

DOCTOR: It's a kind of a... fetal-shaped tumor, Mr. Ortiz-Thurman. *[He sighs out of embarrassment because he didn't need to describe the tumor as "fetal-shaped."*

He damns himself on the inside.]

DAD: God. *[He does the sign of the cross.]* Can you do... surgery?

DOCTOR: Can I ask when you first noticed any change in his behavior?

DAD: Oh, like I said, he's always been a little troubled... You know, with his mom dying during childbirth, he always took it personally for some reason. He takes a lot of things personally.

NURSE: We have a chapel.

DOCTOR: *[He clears his throat as if to shush the nurse because it's too early in the conversation for religion.]* I mean... really odd behavior.

DAD: God. He was twelve when he, one day, tried to hang himself in our basement. *[He lowers his head and takes off the fedora.]* I couldn't believe it. It really came out of nowhere, Doctor. We took him to shrinks, but you think that was the wrong thing to do?

DOCTOR: *[He puts his hand on Dad's shoulder.]* It could've been the tumor.

DAD: So, what about the surgery?

DOCTOR: *[He looks at his expensive shoes.]* I'm afraid it's too late for that. I'm sorry.

NURSE: We're sorry. We have a chapel. We

have refreshments.

DAD: *[He puts his fedora back on and puffs out his chest.]* You make me feel like I did the wrong thing, with the shrinks and all that. Why even ask me those things about when my son showed signs of odd behaviors? Making me realize that, when he committed suicide, I should've brought him to have the inside of his head looked at. And now you say it's too late?

DOCTOR: I'm sorry. *[Again, he frowns because he led Dad down a road of self-reflection and "what ifs."]*

DAD: Tumor? Why fetal-shaped? How long does he have?

As you can imagine, I realize how ironic all this must seem. Perhaps "ironic" is the wrong word—would you agree upon "tragic?" Damn, why did I have to go and have titanium, NEW INTERCOURSE with a girl I made a SUICIDE PACT with in my adolescence whom I didn't remember until she discovered me at a funeral where I was searching for a wife? It's those angelic feet that did me in. Was it worth it? To find a smidgen of love? To be teased with the promise of a sex life? But remember, that wasn't the point. The point was to commit suicides perfectly, and without inexplicably *surviving* and duplicating our corpses. That objective was achieved. Or, I think.

The curtain opens at the foot of my hospital bed—it's Dad and the doctor. The nurse seems to have disappeared which in itself is tragic because I wanted to look at her butt and weep. "Well?" I ask of them as if I don't know my prognosis.

"Son—" the doctor begins to explain, but Dad

interrupts.

"It's a fetal-shaped tumor, D. It's just a matter of days, now. I'm so sorry I didn't catch it sooner. When you committed suicide with the noose, it was the tumor speaking, not your damaged soul. I guess the Lord would not have helped at all." Dad lowers his head in defeat, takes off his fedora and lays it on my bed.

"I'm sorry, son," the doctor says in shame.

Why does the doctor keep calling me "son"? This whole experience of dying from 'natural causes' has been kind of infantilizing. Am I not middle-aged? Isn't my hairline receding? Can't they see that or do they even care? "Well," I say. "So it's not the MULTIPLE SCLEROSIS. I didn't think so because I don't remember anyone ever mentioning that diagnosis to me any time during my life. *Insane?* Definitely. I heard that quite a few times, even from the anorexic psychiatrist who resides inside my head." I try to lift my left head, but I fail. The asymmetry is getting the best of me. "Anyway, I did have a great time inside the MRI. I believe the electromagnetism cured me—of my death-wish, that is, not the fetal-shaped tumor. I guess it can't do anything about that. The MRI simply *illuminated* the tumor and can't shrink it, I guess, since the MRI is just a fancy camera. Did I say it cured me? That I really *do* want to live now?"

Dad doesn't even raise his head to acknowledge me. Perhaps he didn't hear me, or maybe he's even more ashamed that he and the medical establishment didn't predict this deadly predicament and my ultimate demise.

"Did you guys say 'fetal-shaped?'" I ask.

They close the curtain once again to resume their masculine discourse—as if I'm not a man. I hear Dad say that I'm about to start high school. Really? I'm not *that* mentally challenged. A man in his mid-thirties doesn't start high school. I did get a C in Algebra. Don't you see that the ligature marks on my throat are at least twenty-five years old? *Fetal-shaped*, I think. It gets me really wondering. And the curtain opens again. I wish they'd make up their minds if this is the beginning or end of this farce I call my life. Oh, it's the nurse. Yes! *Turn that way*, I want to tell her. *Just a little more... a little more to the left...*

"Hello, D," the nurse says and smiles. Wow, she's black and she's stunning. Not that I'm a racist or anything. I mean, she's quite a sight to be seen. How come I didn't notice she was black before? Maybe it was the double-vision or the asymmetry or the fact that I've been dead and alive and in limbo, time and time again. "My name is Ellen." She reaches out with her left hand and touches my forehead. "Oh, wow," she quietly exclaims. "You have a wound on your temple." She looks at me in the eye and shakes her head. "You didn't do that to yourself, did you?" I shake my head. She turns around and walks toward a cabinet to retrieve some gauze. Her booty is plump and round and bulbous. Gosh, I'm really not in the suicide mode anymore, am I? Golly, I will marry her, too. She's got a beautiful name. I guess I don't need to see her feet because her booty is pretty much a wide screen TV—not in a bad way, or anything, or in a racial way. It's simply a God-thing. That's what happens when you come out of a computer and electromagnetism—you see people in a different light. Not that I wasn't lustful before, but now I can observe and not necessarily *need* to be inside her. I can simply lie here and watch and *be*.

She caresses the exit-wound with antibiotic ointment and a cotton swab. She maneuvers the swab around and around the rim of the wound and I'm pretty much in Heaven again, like when I was inside the MRI. It's not like *going all the way*, but it's pretty damned close. It's definitely not titanium sex in the 21st century. That stuff is for sci-fi perverts, dump trucks, and the new Ozarks. That's why God put a clitoris and a hole in my head. "Is that better?" Ellen asks with a tasteful, call-girl mannerism.

"Yeah, much, much better," I exclaim. My hands are smaller than I remember—pubescent, even. My protuberance is standing, oh yeah, its childish. I guess tumors have a way of turning back the clock of history. It's OK to be entering high school again for the first time, except I'll be dead by the beginning of the semester. I've been dead my whole adult life, so what's the difference? Ellen is about to turn away from me, but I get her attention. "Wait," I say. "Have we met before?" I ask.

She smiles and her grin is like a pot of gold, but not as lame as that simile. Ellen whispers into my working ear, "Are you flirting with me?"

I swallow really hard and blush and my protuberance stands even taller. "I guess," I reply. "Is that bad?" I reach under my blanket and reach for the protuberance without really paying attention.

"No, sweetie," she says, nearly chuckling at this point. "It's just fine." She hovers over me as if she would really like to join me, but Dad and the doctor are right over there. I'm flustered and nearly out of breath, but I manage to ask, "Can you... you know... clean the wound in my head a little more?"

"Sure thing. *Whatever* you want, sweetie."

Ellen. I want to ask her if she has a UTERINE CARBURETOR under her nurse's garb, but that would ruin the mood. I doubt she thought she would find a suitor in Hell, especially on a nice day like this. I'm still going at it under my blanket and she clears her throat, not ceasing to swab the rim of the wound in my head for even one second. "How old are you, sweetie?"

I don't bother to answer. Again, it would ruin the *God-effect*. I imagine she's Elena II, or the first Ellen, or whoever. She's just Nurse Ellen and this is our best chance at a honeymoon before I croak. "Does it really matter?" I ask.

"Well..." she ponders the legality of man and wife, life and death, adult and child. "It doesn't really matter." She smiles again and lifts her skirt simply to show a smidgen of thigh. Ellen, my wife—first with the UTERINE CARBURETOR and my UMBILICAL RECEPTOR and the transmission of the UTERINE BINARY CODE... and now the *real thing*! It's nice, is all I can say, to finally be alive. If it wasn't for the fetal-shaped tumor... but, heck, no more "what ifs." I wouldn't have met Nurse Ellen, my new and final wife, if I wasn't about to croak. And I do know she's *all of the Ellens* in one body. That's it! I committed suicide again—imperfectly, damn it—and I changed Ellen into a parallel-universe Ellen because I couldn't wait for her to jump into the same noose as mine. No matter. I guess I'm going to die the natural way this time—no duplicating corpses or changing Dad's nationality because of my selfish need to kill myself and, then, not actually dying. And it suddenly makes perfect sense! Ellen—the black nurse and my final wife—*is* the same old Ellen from my forgotten childhood SUICIDE PACT *and* the UTERINE CARBURETOR Ellen. Her UTERINE BINARY CODE not only eliminated our ETERNITY GENES, but it impregnated my head! What a weird side-effect of perfecting our suicides, huh? I feel even closer to Nurse Ellen now, especially as *the* climax is about to be endured for the final time. My head is pregnant—not with a fetal-shaped tumor. No! They got it all wrong. From UTERINE BINARY CODE to FETAL MATERIAL TRANSLATION to my daughter, ELENA III! It took all of this suicide, living in limbo, zombies, the MULTIPLE SCLEROSIS, MRIs, and divinity nonsense to finally become a father. If I wasn't dying, they never would've discovered my daughter inside my head. I'm so sorry, ELENA III, that I won't live to guide you through your own life. Don't get depressed or anything like me, OK? I definitely didn't kill myself during your childbirth because I hated your soul or anything. Don't believe that for one minute! As Nurse

Ellen puts the final touches on my wound and I put the final, climactic touches on my other end, I simply want to say goodbye. I love you, ELENA III. And I love you, Dad. And I even love you, too, Mommy. I realize you didn't hate my soul when you died during childbirth. You simply had a terribly small vaginal opening and I barely fit through. It was your massive blood loss and the savage incompetency of the medical establishment that failed you. I'm sorry I blamed you all these years for causing my suicides.

Nurse Ellen caresses the ridge around the hole in my head with her pinky, and I can feel it splitting wide open. You see, the hole in my head is actually *my own tiny vaginal opening* which will hurt really fucking bad when I actually give birth. That's the price you pay for getting pregnant, right, girls? If I had *natural* sex earlier in my life, maybe I'd be a father instead of an INVERTED FATHER-MOTHER. There's no taking back events after perfectly committing suicide—Ellen and I, both. We do share our death and are truly together right here and now, although Nurse Ellen is racially different. Yes, she is my one and only true love! And ELENA III, please don't remember your INVERTED FATHER-MOTHER as a suicidal loon, OK? I'm not leaving you on purpose. It's simply that after my head got pregnant and I'm about to die giving birth to you, the placenta, my bloody mulch, and all my unconscious bullshit through that *tiny vaginal opening in my head*, no one—I mean *absolutely no one*—will ever be able to stuff me back in.

ACKNOWLEDGEMENTS

"History of the Apparatus" and "Recording a Life: Data Transfer Skins" previously appeared in *Fence Magazine*.

"No More Maps" originally appeared in *Drunken Boat*.

"The Helter-Skelter War" and "Extinguish the Light" originally appeared in *Steel Toe Review*.

"Grief!" originally appeared in the *KGB Bar Lit Journal*.

"End Tram" originally appeared in *Dark Sky Magazine*.

"Food" originally appeared in *Georgetown Review*.

"The Blue Dot" originally appeared in *Open City*.

"Shelter" originally appeared in *Monkey Bicycle*.

All other stories are original to this collection.

ABOUT THE AUTHOR

Leland Pitts-Gonzalez earned an MFA in writing from Columbia University and published his first novel *The Blood Poetry* (Raw Dog Screaming Press) in 2012. His short fiction has appeared in various literary journals. He lives in Queens, New York.

CATALOGUE BLUE 555

CB555-01: 555 Vol. 1: None So Worthy
CB555-02: The Book of Adventures
CB555-03: Mr. Malin and the Night
CB555-04: Haiku Fuck You
CB555-05: 555 Vol. 2: This Head, These Limbs
CB555-06: The Book of Adventures 2
CB555-07: A Terrible Thing
CB555-08: 555 Vol. 3: Questions & Cancers
CB555-09: Savage Anesthesia

Forthcoming:
CB555-10: Plague Gods

www.ingramcontent.com/pod-product-compliance
Lightning Source LLC
Chambersburg PA
CBHW021011120726
47905CB00009B/2962

* 9 7 8 0 9 9 6 2 7 6 8 4 9 *